While The Angels Slept

DEL GARRETT

Published by

Raven's Inn Press
806 Rhoden Rd.
Judsonia, AR 72081

Copyright 2011 by B. Odell Garrett

ISBN: 978-0-615-52225-8

First Edition
September 2011
Shadow Light Press

Second Edition
October 2015
Raven's Inn Press

Cover Image Courtesy of
Simon Howden at FreeDigitalPhotos.net

Dedication

To my darling niece Betty Thompson Woodward, who is a couple years older than me and who has always looked after me and loved me without question. Besides my wife, my children and grandchildren, she is the closest family member I have and perhaps the only one who shares the boldness of the generation from which we sprang. We are products of the days of Camelot when the American spirit was adventurous enough to travel to the moon. The art, literature, music and all things red, white and blue and the spirituality of One Nation Under God are the things that made me who I am today, and I'm sure she feels the same about herself. She has done some writing of her own but prefers to read my stories than to compete with me. I love her dearly.

While The Angels Slept

Chapter 1

TWILIGHT HAD FALLEN over the Paris skyline. The last golden rays of sunlight dipped below the horizon, yielding their majesty to a dusty purple sky dotted here and there with the first spattering of early summer stars that spread slowly across the heavens. As these diamond-like jewels of the sky spread their glitter over the Paris Museum of Modern Art a lone figure dressed all in black waited in the shadows across the Seine river at the edge of the *Garden of Champ de Mars*, otherwise known as Eiffel Park. Fully lighted, the Eiffel Tower, the main tourist attraction in Paris, loomed dramatically above him in the background, but held no interest for the man. Crouched beneath a maple tree, Pietro Fanucci chain smoked from a nearly empty pack of Gitanes Brunes, a dark-papered cigarette with a strong flavor and aroma.

He had watched the museum from the time its lights had turned on and waited until he knew the building would be closed to the public before he crushed out his last cigarette, looked for a fresh one inside the pack and shrugged his shoulders when he found it was empty. He crumpled the pack and threw it on the ground. He stood up slowly and stretched the stiffness out of his body. Feeling better, he strode past the wharf along the

Quai d'Orsay and headed for the other side of the river.

This was not the best weather to be breaking into a museum in the middle of the night. Early May had been better, sunny with daytime temperatures in the eighties, but here on the twenticth of May heavy rain had fallen across most of France causing the nights to be quite chilly. He was two weeks away from his thirty-eighth birthday, still a young man but old enough to feel the first pangs of arthritis creeping into his joints. The weather didn't help the stiffness feel any better.

Pietro shoved his hands inside his coat pockets and trudged along the pathway leading out of the park, As he neared the bridge he had to cross to reach his destination he looked left and right for traffic and was satisfied to find none. His mission was starting well enough even with the chilly weather. Pietro could not carry out his plans before this night because of Museum Day, the annual open house in which museum patrons could visit for free and the museum stayed open later than usual to accommodate the influx of visitors. The paintings he intended to steal tonight were amongst the most valued and most admired masterpieces in the museum's collection and were, thusly, some of the best guarded paintings on display. No, Pietro had had to wait until Museum Day was over and security was back to normal and no one would be expecting a burglary.

Pietro had planned this heist for two months,

even applying for a position as an electrician with the museum which gave him access to the alarm systems and made it easy for him to disarm them. He had just that morning disabled part of the system which protected a window in the eastern wing of the building. The window was not in the main stream of traffic, so the location made it perfect for his choice of after-hours entry. Bypassing only this window, he made sure the rest of the alarm system worked normally because one of the three guards on duty was sure to check the main alarm as he locked the doors for the night. Pietro wasn't worried. He'd been a top-rated electrician before becoming a burglar. From the window where he would enter, it would be a simple matter for him to disarm the rest of the system once he was inside.

As Pietro reached the bridge, he noticed several lovers strolling toward him. Trays of flowers waited beside the bridge to be planted the next day. All over the city, planting day was just around the corner. The tourist season was at hand and city officials wanted its main attractions to reflect the beauty of their beloved Paris. One young couple stopped to admire the rows of flowers. Pietro stopped at the edge of the bridge and waited for them to pass out of sight before he moved forward.

"Oh, *si belle,* so beautiful," the girl said as the couple strolled past a box of flowers.

"Not as pretty as you," her lover said.

Crossing the bridge, Pietro stopped suddenly

half-way with nowhere to turn. Coming at him, two police cars blared their sirens and flashed their lights, most probably in response to a call from their dispatcher. *Were they coming for him?* Pietro couldn't imagine how the police would have known what he was planning. He needn't worry, though. The patrol cars sped past him without a glance his way. He breathed a sigh of relief and reached in his pocket for another cigarette. His hand came away empty as he remembered crushing the pack under the tree at Eiffel Park. He cursed under his breath and moved quickly at an angle to 11 Avenue du President Wilson where the museum stood waiting for him. He approached the east wing quietly, staying deep within the shadows of the building and bushes, anything that would allow him to blend in with the night.

He withdrew a small rubber hammer from his jacket pocket and broke the window. He listened carefully to make sure his handiwork on the alarm system had been successful. Reaching inside carefully he found the clasp and slid it open, then lifted the frame and brushed away the broken glass on the window sill. Once inside, he carefully lowered the window in case someone should walk by and notice it open. He pulled his hood over his head. He had been successful in overcoming the alarm system, but he knew the security cameras were bound to capture his image as he walked around inside and the raised hood would cover his face to protect his identity. He only needed a few hours to complete his mission and get away long enough to reach the docks where he had left a large fishing boat tied to the dock to carry him across the sea to England. From there, he had arranged air transportation to Canada..

Throughout the night Pietro went about the business of picking only certain masterpieces, those which had already been advertised and delivery guaranteed to art lovers who wanted the pieces for their private collections—those that hung on the wall in private dens under lock and key and nobody ever got the chance to admire them but their owners. Those collectors didn't care if the paintings were stolen, only that they now belonged to them.

Of course, many of those collectors would never know that the paintings they purchased in the days to come were not the real masterpieces. Waiting in America, a very talented forger was ready to copy the paintings and the man who had financed this operation would pass them off as the originals—the more copies the forger made, the more money Pietro and his benefactor would make. There really is no honor among thieves.

Pietro carefully removed each painting from its frame, six paintings in all. He did not want to destroy them by cutting them out of their frames. This way, they could be reframed as they were originally seen for the man who had hired him. He knew that only a few of those socialite collectors might know the real thing when they saw it but his contact in California was a man of great fortune and great knowledge when it came to fine art. It would be he, the man financing the operation, who would retain the real masterpieces.

Several times Pietro heard one of the guards' footsteps in the outer hallway. He wasn't worried. He knew the guard would be in a hurry to return to his station. Tonight was the guards' weekly card game. The guards would play all night long for a few cents a hand, never betting higher than two euros.

The last guard of the morning shift strolled by singing a popular tune containing the words, 'It's Too Late,' to which Pietro replied, "*Oui, Mon ami*. It's too late to stop me now. Tonight we are making history."

The clock chimed six of a morning when Pietro left the building. He had eluded both the alarms and the security cameras which, even though they had caught him going about his business, the images of him stealing the paintings had not yet been noticed by the guards who were wrapping up their card game and wiping the sleep from their eyes. Pietro had rolled up the six paintings inside wrappings of oilcloth and made his way back to the east wing of the building where he opened the window and shoved the paintings through, letting them drop to the dew covered ground below. Pietro climbed out into the early morning fog coming from over the river and retrieved the paintings. Like a ghost, he disappeared within the fog and made his way to a spot in Eiffel Park where he had hidden a bicycle to ride the long distance to where his fishing vessel waited.

The theft was discovered an hour later. The guards, much to their embarrassment, reported the theft to their superiors who, in turn, called the police. The *Brigade de Répression du Banditisme,* a special unit of the French Police, discovered the broken window at the rear of the east wing and a busted padlock off a grille giving access to the interior of the museum. They immediately sealed off the building.

Patrons wishing to enter the museum that day were greeted with a sign hastily hung on the ornate bronze front doors that said the museum was closed due to 'technical difficulties.'

Chapter 2

H E WAS ON TOP OF HER AGAIN. Lydia's husband held her down with one hand and grabbed the front of her soft pink silk blouse with his other, ripping the material from her body along with the crème-colored lace bra that she wore underneath. She felt the cool night air rush over her breasts, sending prickles along her bare skin, causing her nipples to rise unwillingly. Her husband pressed his face close to hers. She smelled bourbon and cigar tobacco on his breath and the salty odor of sweat coming from his body. The perspiration covering his body matted the fine hairs on the front of his deeply tanned chest, it made her own skin feel clammy. She tried to push him off of her but even in his drunken state he was simply too strong for her. He shoved himself between her legs. Reaching one hand down past the flat surface of her stomach, he shredded the lace panties that matched her bra and pulled them from her body. He threw the panties to one side and crawled deeper upon the bed. He settled his muscular body more solidly between her legs and guided himself into the soft folds of her flesh. He heaved himself forward in the initial thrust of his assault and held her down tightly against the sheet and mattress as he took what he wanted from her.

The stubble of beard on his chin raked harshly against her delicate flesh, burning the soft surfaces of her face and neck as if he were scraping her with course sandpaper. Her skin reddened, her body jerked under his thrusts. But the fight in her was over. She knew it would not matter, nothing would matter, not when her husband was this drunk and this demanding.

The ordeal, as unpleasant as it was for her, had become routine in the first few months of marriage and, therefore, was physically less irritating with each attack. Her mental anguish was another matter. She closed her eyes and concentrated on the scent of flowers that wafted through the open French doors of their bedroom, gently floating upon the nightly breeze that was cool and comforting to her bare skin. It had rained earlier that day and the smell of fresh dirt mingled with the mixture of perfumes rising from the flower bed in the patio outside, fragrant hyacinths in pink, lavender and blue colors, white gardenias, blue Cleveland sage and the sweet incense of the Jeffrey Pine lulled her senses and helped her endure the moment with her husband. In the morning, because of his drinking, he wouldn't remember what he had done tonight; or if he somehow did, he would apologize, open his hand-tooled leather wallet and hand her three crisp one-hundred dollar bills and tell her to buy a new blouse. To Josh Taylor, money was the answer to all the problems in the world.

A little voice inside her told Lydia to be reasonable. After all, Josh was her husband. Married couples were supposed to be intimate with each other. But this kind of lovemaking never felt right to her. *Lovemaking?* There was nothing about the way Josh manhandled her like this that could be called love.

What seemed so strange to Lydia is that she had married him because he *was* so powerful. *How could I like someone so powerful, yet hate the way he treats me?* Her husband epitomized the young upwardly mobile, go-for-broke and grab-all-the-gusto you can kind of man who was, like her father, a leader instead of a follower, the kind of man she thought she wanted. Josh had risen quickly in his profession. An engineer, he built buildings—huge structures with massive domes and steeples that stretched upwards to the clouds, wonderful skyscrapers that captured both the magnitude of modern architecture and the pristine beauty of angular lines that dominated the skyline and made Josh Taylor a name to remember; no, not just a name, a legend among his peers—and, of course, made him rich in the process.

He had money enough to buy her a hundred new blouses, a thousand, whatever she wanted. He could buy her the whole damn store if she wanted it. When you have tons of money, it doesn't matter how much you have. Being rich simply meant he could follow his dreams without worrying about where he would get the funding. What Lydia wanted more than money was tenderness coupled with passion, but Josh had his dark side, like now, as he pawed at her breasts and smothered her mouth with his unwanted kisses. This was not what she had dreamed marriage to him would be like. She closed her eyes and let him have his way with her. She forced herself to become so detached that she didn't even notice Josh's final shout of relief.

When it was over, Lydia picked herself up off the bed and tiptoed to the bathroom so she would not wake him. He lay naked upon the bed, lost in his drunken stupor, while she ran a hot bath, adding her crystal salts and oil beads, and watching the water turn blue and bubbly. She looked in the mirror and winced at the rash on her face and neck where his beard had scraped her. She shrugged her shoulders. The redness would disappear, she told herself. It had happened before. It would happen again. She stepped into the tub to soak away the bruises Josh had inflicted upon her where he held her too tightly. She took her time, knowing that he would still be asleep when she finished her bath. She eventually stepped out of the tub when the water had cooled down and dried herself off with a big fluffy pink towel. She crawled onto her side of the bed and covered herself with just a sheet. In the morning, the sun would shine brightly through the lace curtains, the morning air would smell fresh through the open window. She would change the sheets and forget how they smelled of his sweat from the night before. All would be right in the world again. Josh would get dressed, give her a loving kiss—even if his lips still tasted of bourbon and stale cigars—and he would tell her how much he loved her.

She would believe him, of course. She always did, because when he was sober Josh was a loving husband and good provider and he'd do anything for her. But the growing pattern of domination had repeated itself so many times that she knew what to expect each time he started drinking.

It was morning. Josh stuck his head out of the bathroom, lather covering half his face, the other side shaved clean already, and told her there was a party at the Atherton's that night. More drinking, more working the crowds, more using her to enlist and entice prospective male investors.

"Be ready by six," he said. "We don't want to be late. And wear something especially sexy."

That meant he wanted her to show a lot of cleavage, something she had no trouble doing. At five feet four inches, she'd always been what her mother called top heavy. Ever since she had developed her figure, starting at age thirteen, she had attracted male glances. Always popular with the boys, Lydia was also self-conscious of her good looks and didn't feel any better about herself until one of her girlfriends prompted her to try out for the cheerleading squad. Lydia knew she wasn't the smartest girl in school, the grades on her report card were proof of that. But being accepted for the cheerleading squad helped boost her confidence and her popularity. She moved naturally and gracefully. She had no problem showing off her charms on the football field or now at any of the parties she and Josh attended. Besides, she liked the way she looked. Her clothes were expensive, the latest fashions. Josh saw to it that she had the best of everything. Her dresses accentuated her beauty and even the more revealing ones never made her feel cheap. She drew the attention of those men to whom Josh would introduce himself. With his easy going personality he never failed to turn the conversation from being about his wife to the subject of his business and how they could invest in it.

Lady Atherton—a real lady; they were British—was a darling at seventy-one; her husband, Raymond—he preferred to be called by his first name instead of his title—was equally charming at seventy-four. He reminded Lydia of the actor, Fred Astaire, so dapper in his dress, so cordial in his smile and conversation. She enjoyed the Athertons and always looked forward to seeing them, even though she had little background in common with them. No titles in her family, no inclusion in *Who's Who in America*. Lydia's role was that of arm decoration for her husband. She knew that and accepted it. She was certainly pretty enough with her golden-blonde curls, blue-green eyes, and perfectly white teeth. She had done some modeling, enough so that she was used to people staring at her. Women, for their envy; men, with their openly lusty gazes. Josh never acted jealous when men flocked around her. They were usually the piggy banks from which he drew his income. He asked little more of his wife than to smile and be gracious among those he courted for business or the motion picture and Broadway superstars he enjoyed being seen with, and told her to watch her posture when the photographers snapped their pictures for the society pages of the Los Angeles Times.

Lydia played her part well because, deep down, she enjoyed meeting all of Josh's friends and others, people whose names and faces she saw regularly in the news, gossip columns, and on television or on the big screen. Josh, besides always dressing her in the latest fashions, always provided her with stunning jewelry, a new necklace for each party, and insisted that she make regular visits to Maxine's, the best salon in town. What woman wouldn't like that kind of lavish lifestyle?

She spent the whole day getting ready. She chose a long, flowing black dress with a deep 'V' cut in front held up by spaghetti straps. She wore Christian Dior patent leather shoes with a small black bow in front and only a short heel. A simple, delicate golden chain around her neck extended low enough so the diamond and ruby pendent on it rested provocatively above the start of her glorious cleavage.

By five that evening, Lydia could have walked the red carpet in Hollywood. The only problem was she had no escort. Josh had not yet arrived, nor had he called. Lydia started to worry. She turned on the television to catch the news, but the only item being reported was a theft of some valuable paintings from a museum in Paris.

At five-thirty, her very inebriated husband showed up and announced they were not going to the party. Lydia, whose temper rarely surfaced, looked at herself in the hallway mirror and did something she never expected doing. She threw her purse at Josh and cursed at him.

"You *bastard!*"

To his credit, Josh could sober up instantly when he had to. This was one of those moments.

"I spent the whole day getting ready for this party and you spent your day getting drunk with your friends. The Athertons are nice people and I don't want to disappoint them. And I don't have to remind you that a good many of your business contacts wouldn't have pulled out their checkbooks for you without Raymond's endorsement. You owe him."

Josh straightened his suit and tie, stretched his neck uncomfortably and looked his wife in the eye. "My dear, you are perfectly correct and I shall be ready to go in just a moment."

He excused himself to the bathroom where he doused cold water on his face, ran a razor over the five o'clock shadow on his chin and jaw line, and ran his fingers through the dark locks of his hair that forever hung down across his eyes. His boyish good looks charmed both the men and the ladies every bit as much as Lydia's girl-next-door features and pin-up model body charmed the men and made their wives twitch with jealousy.

A quick change into his tuxedo and a splash of British Sterling on his face and Josh presented himself to Lydia, who by this time was feeling a tremor run up and down her body, aghast at the thought of previously raising her voice to her husband. But it had the right effect, she thought, because Josh's face stretched into a slightly skewed smile that made him look even more boyish and more charming than usual.

"I'll drive," he announced as they stepped outside.

"How many drinks have you had?"

"Not enough to worry about, I assure you." The smile convinced her because at their young age—he was barely twenty-eight and she was twenty-two—they had yet to learn that alcohol and gasoline make a lousy cocktail.

Chapter 3

J OSH NAVIGATED THE ROLLING HILLS well enough, pushing the classic Mercedes Gullwing faster and faster. Lydia sat nervously throughout the short drive to the Atherton's. Knowing her husband had been drinking, and would continue to do so at the party, she worried about their trip home afterward.

Reaching the entrance to the Atherton's residence, Josh headed up the straight drive until he caught the turn at the loop that served as a circular driveway in front of the house. The straight portion ran all the way to the back of the house where two double-door garages housed a line of vintage cars. It was through his association with Raymond Atherton that Josh had found and purchased the Mercedes sports car he loved so much. He parked the car and turned off the engine.

"Maybe you'd better let me have the keys," Lydia suggested. She held out her hand but Josh only sneered at her and stepped out of the car.

"I told you I'm okay." Josh slammed shut the door of the Mercedes and stormed toward the house, leaving Lydia to follow after him. They had arrived at the party along with two other couples so their lateness went mostly unnoticed. They were met at the door by James Austin, the Atherton's assistant. That was how Raymond referred to him. He never used the terms butler or servant because he felt those were demeaning to the man. Austin smiled and directed them to the den where Lord and Lady Atherton were greeting their guests. Once inside the hallway, Josh's hand guided Lydia's elbow as they entered the wood paneled den. Gone was the angered look on his face she had seen earlier. He had replaced it with a warm smile and a look that made his eyes sparkle. Everywhere they looked people responded to Josh's smile. He had that kind of charm that made his presence acceptable to both men and women.

In the den, on its dark walls, hung a collection of paintings and family photographs. Many of the photos were in black and white from when the Athertons were much younger. Some of them depicted Raymond on safari; some of the trophies of those hunts also decorated the room. Hanging on the walls were the heads of a gazelle from the Namibia Kahalari Desert in South Africa and two Big Horn sheep from Montana. A stuffed Kodiak bear from Alaska stood out of the way in one corner of the room intimidating the guests with its sheer size. Josh and Lydia circled the room, taking into consideration who was there and which pocket book might soon be opened for Josh's latest venture, a strip mall he was building in a busy downtown Los Angeles shopping district.

But this party wasn't for Josh. The Athertons had acquired another work of art by a grand master to add to their collection. Raymond was himself an artist and more than a few of the canvases on the walls bore his own signature. But his hobby was collecting and selling art, and tonight he had on display in front of the fireplace a charcoal sketch he said was the work of Jacques-Louis David, a study in the year 1800 by the artist in preparation for his famous painting of Madame Récamier. In the sketch, *la madame* was reclining in the same manner as she does in the finished painting. The sketch was only two feet long. The original painting stretches a full eight feet across and five feet, nine inches high. The artist used only a few props: a divan, step stool and an oil lamp on a long pole. Raymond had placed a photo of the original painting on the table near the charcoal sketch along with a card which he propped up against the frame indicating his willingness to sell the sketch for a mere thirty-five thousand dollars.

"There is money to be made in the scraps of paper these artists often threw away," Raymond told Josh. "The trick is finding it and buying it for a ridiculously low sum of money. The profits can be outstandingly substantial."

Admirers looked at the sketch but passed it by, savoring the *hors d'oeuvres* and wine and small talk among the other guests. Lydia joined them, smiling in such a way that it looked almost genuine. The maid, Betty, appeared beside her with a cocktail on a tray. Lydia took the drink and listened to what the others were saying. These were movie people so their talk centered around what movies were being shot by Eastwood, Tarantino or Spielberg. She enjoyed these people, but she knew well enough that she would be doing her own acting in a few minutes when Josh wanted her to make her rounds, widen her lips, show more teeth, and add an extra sparkle to her eyes. She knew what he wanted and always played her part well, knowing exactly when to hold her welcoming hug a little tighter and a little longer than natural when Josh introduced her to his prospective investors. Lydia didn't mind. She thought she was helping her husband, and she did enjoy the money he made. If her performance helped him seal a deal, she was all for it. Josh didn't care for the art Raymond offered, but he knew that before the night was over the old man was sure to pocket a fat check for it and be happy enough to steer some of the wealth in Josh's direction.

Both of the Athertons remained stationary throughout the reception, she in a pink chiffon dress with a full skirt, dusty in color, and cut in a tea gown length, The waistband was adorned on the left side with a black patent leather belt and a white dahlia made of silk. Her Christian Dior patent leather pumps matched her belt and complimented the dusty pink color of the dress. Lady Atherton stood under a giant oil painting of herself when she was younger. Raymond stood beside the fireplace where his brown woolen sweater, Hush Puppy slippers and the dark burled pipe in his mouth enhanced his country gentleman image. They let the party goers come to them, whether it was by design as lord and lady of the estate, or if in their golden years they found that moving about exacerbated their arthritis too much.

The party looked successful to Lydia, as parties go, but she worried about her husband's drinking. James and Betty Austin roamed freely amongst the guests, providing a variety of drinks. He served as bartender and both he and his wife smiled politely as she served the drinks all around. They were the only servants in the Atherton house.

Josh seemed to be keeping a miraculous control on his behavior throughout the evening, although she knew he'd had quite a few drinks before the party, and even more during it. He dined in small amounts, preferring conversation to cholesterol.

The food was rich in flavor: two choices of meats, roast beef and a Hawaiian ham, a favorite of the host. Freshly steamed vegetables made enticingly more delicious by a caterer who knew just the right amount of cheese sauce to drip over them or wine sauce in which to sauté the others…and the desserts were irresistible…Lydia made sure she tried the chocolate cake topped with strawberries and dark chocolate icing. She might regret this choice in the morning when she stepped on the scales, but tonight she threw caution to the wind and devoured the dreamy concoction with a smile and a smear of chocolate on her lips.

Meanwhile, Josh excused himself along with a few of the other men to step outside and smoke a cigar. Lady Atherton tolerated her husband's pipe and Black Cavendish tobacco because he liked the blend so well and because he smoked his pipe only on occasion. Regular pipe and cigar smokers, and especially those who smoked common cigarettes, she relegated to the patio outside where they could puff away to their hearts content and the double French doors were sealed well enough to protect the house from the bitter odor of their caustic fumes.

More drinks followed as all the smokers indulged in their frivolity and discussed business ventures. Josh handed his business cards to all of the men and Raymond patted him on the back, sort of a passing of the lance from the days of knighthood, showing his approval of the young man.

Lydia endured the usual comments from older women about how handsome her husband looked in his tuxedo. One woman, who had shown too much fondness for champagne, made a remark about how handsome Josh might look *out* of his tuxedo. Her comment was quickly swept away by a more sensitive partygoer, one who complimented Lydia on her dress for the evening.

In all, it was a good party but Lydia was glad when it started winding down. Josh was still in a good mood and, with business out of the way, he noticed Lydia as if she were the prom queen and he the prom king. His comments to her, spoken rather loudly she thought due to his drinking, were filled with sexual innuendo and she knew he would be wanting to leave soon.

They made their final rounds, saying goodbye to everyone.

"I had a wonderful time, as always," she told Lady Atherton.

"Thank you, my dear. You are a charming young girl. You remind me of me when I was your age." Lady Atherton looked wincingly at her portrait. "Raymond swept me off my feet when I was about your age. I've been the happiest woman in the world since then. I'm sure you feel the same way about your husband."

Lydia paused only a second before answering. She hoped it had not been noticeable. "Yes, Josh is both loving and a good provider. I adore him as much as you adore your husband."

Lady Atherton also gave a pause, one that Lydia immediately noticed, before smiling and patting Lydia on the shoulder. "We married well, both of us, didn't we? We must always support our husbands by being there for them."

It was a strange comment, Lydia thought, one in which she felt that Lady Atherton was trying to tell her something, acknowledgment of a deeper meaning and understanding between two women who shared a secret. Lady Atherton smiled in her usual elegant manner as she bid farewell to Lydia and turned to say goodnight to her next guest.

"Are you sure you're okay to drive?" Lydia

paused at the door of their Mercedes before getting in. Josh looked across the top of the car at her and an angry bolt of lightning flashed in his eyes.

"Get in the damn car, Lydia. I told you before that I was fine. Don't keep on. And smile...."

One of the couples that had sat next to them at dinner strolled past and waved a cheery goodnight to them. Josh's bleached white teeth flashed like a beacon in the darkness as he pumped the man's hand furiously before letting go.

"I'll call you tomorrow," the man said, holding up Josh's business card as if to assure him he hadn't lost it.

"Better make it after nine," Josh said. "I'll be busy in the morning." He leered at Lydia and smiled back at the couple. The man laughed and looked at Lydia with a knowing glance. The woman smiled and kept her eyes on Josh. They walked toward their own car and Josh nodded at Lydia to get in the Mercedes.

"You look ravishing tonight," he said, but kept his gaze on the rear view mirror.

"Thank you," she replied, quietly.

"You know, that old queer hooked me up tonight with about half a million dollars."

"Old queer?"

"Raymond. Come on, don't tell me he has you fooled, too. He's as homo as they come; well, maybe bisexual might be the proper choice of words; but nevertheless, he chatted up a few of the guys tonight who will probably become good friends with him in the future."

"You don't mean...."

"Yes, that's exactly what I *do* mean. Don't worry, he had the good sense not to try that with me when we first met. I think the old queen actually likes me as a friend. But he's also using me. I have the charisma to draw people into my web. He's content just to hide in the shadows and pick and choose which of these party animals might be interested in his little games. Besides, he gets a good return off what I make. So it evens out in the long run. He's using me and I'm using him. *Muy simpatico.*"

"Oh, I don't believe you, about him being queer I mean."

"That's 'cause you're a naïve, little school girl who has never been exposed to what really goes on in the world. That's okay, just keep smiling at the men and shake your butt a little when you walk around them. If they like what they see, and believe me they will, they'll want to know us better and that means going into business with me or inviting us to their own parties where I can always find new suckers to fleece out of their money."

"But you don't take advantage of them."

"No, not really. I've never run any scams. Everything I do makes money and anyone who invests with me will get a righteous return on their investment. It just means I can build any damn thing I want and always use somebody else's money doing it. That's business, sweetheart. Don't ever forget that."

Josh kicked over the Mercedes' engine and roared out of the circular driveway. From Eagle Vista Drive he took the Santa Monica Freeway to the Pacific Coast Highway. When Lydia asked him why he was going in the wrong direction he said he had a surprise for her. So he took the long way home. It meant going by the ocean, which he always liked to do on nights like this with a full moon sitting high in a cloud-covered sky and the salty smell of the Pacific sea spray sprinkling his face through the open window of the sports car; nights like this, when the warm Santa Ana wind blew in from the south and the moonlight twinkled over the waves, like so many diamonds rolling across a robe of black velvet that rippled in soft argental patterns when you brushed your hand over it. He went all the way to Washington Boulevard and cut down toward Marina del Ray. He stopped the Mercedes near the landing outside the marina but did not get out of the car.

"Look at it," he said, pointing toward a sleek, new thirty-two foot cruiser tied up at the pier. "She's a little slower than some boats, but easy enough to control, even in choppy waters. She'll do about seven knots with the wind behind her."

"You bought a sailboat?"

"Say hello to *Lady Lydia*. She's going to be our vacation getaway this year. Lots of room on her, you'll enjoy how she sails." He turned on the radio to some soft music as they sat there admiring the yacht. Tony Bennett's *I Left My Heart In San Francisco* gave way to a news flash about six paintings which had been stolen from the Museum of Modern Art in Paris.

"Thieves broke a window and crept through in the wee hours of the morning," the reporter said. *"They removed the six paintings from their frames and escaped undetected. Taken in the heist were* Le pigeon aux petits pois *by Pablo Picasso,* La Pastorale *by Henri Matisse,* L'Olivier Près de l'Estaque *by George Braque,* La Femme à l'éventail *by Amedeo Modigliani,* Nature Morte aux Chandeliers *by Fernand Léger and* Monk by the Sea *by Caspar David Fredrich, which was on loan from the Alte Nationalgalerie in Berlin. The paintings were valued at one hundred million euros, nearly one hundred twenty-three million in U.S. dollars."*

Josh turned off the radio and eased the Mercedes out of the parking lane and turned left onto the San Diego Freeway, then turned right onto Venice Boulevard and reconnected with the Santa Monica Freeway heading home. He drove fast. The Mercedes hummed like the purring of a large cat as its speedometer climbed higher and higher. Lydia felt a tingle of fear race up her spine as her pulse rose along with the needle on the speedometer. She clutched the edge of her seat with her right hand and placed her left hand on Josh's thigh.

"Please, not so fast," she whispered.

"Hon, don't ever tell me how to drive," he

shot back at her. His foot stepped heavier on the gas peddle and the Mercedes negotiated the twists and turns in the road with ease.

"Please—"

Her voice fell silent as she saw the car in front of them, moving along at the speed limit, making it look as if it had stopped in the road because of the rate of speed the Mercedes was going. Josh saw it, too, and jerked on the wheel. The Mercedes swerved around the other car and returned to the right hand lane as smoothly as if being driven by a race car driver. Josh was no race car driver, but tonight he and the Mercedes blended together, man and machine.

He looked across at Lydia who sat frozen with her hand on his leg. Her eyes stared straight ahead in an open wideness of fear. Her right hand gripped the edge of her seat so tightly the blood drained from her flesh, her perfectly sexy body that usually slumped a bit now sat upright in perfect posture. Josh felt the increased pressure on his thigh and his thoughts left the road for a moment as his eyes took in the large roundness of his wife's breasts as they rose and fell in synchronized rhythm with the way she was breathing. His pulse quickened and his hands tightened their grip on the steering wheel.

A large bird slammed into the front windshield. The glass cracked with a loud, popping sound, and a blood smear spread across the broken glass. Josh's tight grip yanked the steering wheel to the right. Lydia's seat belt dug sharply into her stomach and she wedged herself as far as she could against the back of her seat. She screamed. The Mercedes zigged and zagged across the highway, its wheels coming dangerously close to the edge of the road on the left side, then zipping across the highway to the construction site guardrail on the right.

A loud screeching noise filled Lydia's ears as the car hit the guardrail and her world rolled topsy-turvy around her as the Mercedes flipped over, spinning upside down in a clockwise pattern in the middle of the highway. Had it continued spinning, Josh and Lydia might have been safe inside the well-built compartment. Instead, the car behind them couldn't stop in time and hit the rear bumper of their vehicle, causing it to skid sideways along the asphalt. Josh's door ripped off its hinges and sparks flew all around them like a handful of giant sparklers at a Fourth of July picnic. The Mercedes stopped skidding and rotated in a slow spin that wound its way down to a halt.

The driver of the other vehicle got out and ran to Josh and Lydia's car. A moment later, an oncoming electrical utility truck pulled to a stop with its headlights fixed on the Mercedes. The light glared inside the crushed compartment giving Lydia a stark view of her husband whose hands still gripped the steering wheel. She called his name but he didn't answer. They were upside down and Josh's head dangled in place, his eyes open in a fearful stare, She reached her hand over to his neck and felt the warm, sticky liquid covering his flesh. When one of the drivers yanked open Lydia's door, a heavy scraping sound drowned out Lydia's scream. The Mercedes' lights came on inside and she could tell from the way Josh's bloody head swung back and forth without support that his neck was broken. She screamed again and passed out.

Chapter 4

L YDIA AWOKE IN A HOSPITAL ROOM to a blinding light piercing her one open eye, her left eye was covered by a heavy bandage. A white cotton portable curtain surrounded her bed and an IV dripped saline solution into her arm. She tried to read the bag, but could only make out the largest lettering: *Sodium Chloride, 0.9%.*

"It's just to keep you from dehydrating." A young, black nurse smiled at Lydia and fastened the end panels of the curtain to reduce the amount of light coming in.

Do they teach that smile in nursing school?

The nurse wore a loose fitting light blue top with large, square pockets and matching pants. A white and flowered cap stretched across the top of her head. She leaned over the bed and slipped a pressure clamp over Lydia's left index finger. "How are we feeling today?" The nurse flipped a switch on a table top monitor and Lydia felt the clamp on her finger tighten slightly. A moment later a pulse rate showed on the large screen of the patient monitor. The nurse printed out a reading and retrieved the clamp, placing it and its umbilical line on the tray in front of the machine.

"Your blood pressure is fine, a little low but that's because of the medicines they gave you when you came into the trauma unit. The doctor will come by in a moment to check on you."

"What about my husband?" Lydia already knew the answer, but hoped she might be wrong.

"The doctor will be here in a moment. Just rest a little more." The nurse patted Lydia on the arm, but the look in the woman's eyes confirmed what Lydia already knew. Josh was dead. Her last image of him looking like Lon Chaney, Sr., in *Phantom of the Opera* came back to haunt her. She dropped her head back on the pillow and closed her eye to stem the flood of tears she knew would still come sooner or later. She preferred later because she didn't think she could handle it right now, even with the painkillers taking control of her body. It was her mind that hurt, her mind and her heart, not the physical injuries she'd sustained, but the ones that would stay with her long after she was released from the hospital.

The doctor arrived a few minutes after the nurse had left. Looking like those you see on television, he stood there with his light brown hair neatly combed, his face and neck showing a good tan and he had a smile so white you'd swear he moonlighted for toothpaste commercials on television. And why not? After all, this was Los Angeles where everybody wanted to be an actor. He introduced himself as Doctor Shaner, checked Lydia's chart and the printout of the blood pressure check the nurse had just taken.

He smiled the same hospital smile at Lydia. *They do teach that smile in med school.* Doctor Shaner asked her the same question, "How are you feeling?" She wanted to say she felt like crap, like she'd just been pushed through a meat grinder and that every nerve in her body was on fire. She nodded, instead, giving him a weak smile. "You're a very lucky lady," the doctor said, as he adjusted his stethoscope and warmed the disk at the end of it before slipping it inside the top of her gown. "No bones broken, a few minor cuts and abrasions is all. And your lungs are clear," he said, removing the stethoscope. "The worst of it was a piece of glass we removed from your eye. No serious damage there, it won't affect your vision. We'll remove the bandage tomorrow."

"My husband is dead, isn't he?"

Doctor Shaner paused before answering. "I'm sorry for your loss." He placed a hand on Lydia's shoulder in a gesture of sincere sorrow.

Just like on TV, he's going to tell me that they did everything they could do to save him but, try as they might, we all have to answer to a greater power.

"There was nothing we could do. Take comfort, if you can, that your husband did not suffer for long. His death was instantaneous."

Lydia closed her good eye as another tear rolled down her cheek. She leaned her head back on the crisp white pillow and clutched the sheets tightly around her. She didn't hear the doctor leave. When the nurse returned with more painkillers, Lydia took them without question. They worked quickly, sending her into a floating haze that robbed her of any feeling and, *bless me all to hell*, she thought, did not let her mind recreate any images about the accident or what life would be like without Josh by her side.

The day went as quickly as it came. Occasional chatter outside drew her attention as the sleeping pills wore off, but only briefly. The pills had done their job. She drifted in and out of consciousness a bit before finally waking up. A food tray had been placed near her while she slept. The entrée was still warm when she uncovered the plate. She smelled the chicken patty before she saw it. Slow grilled and smothered in white gravy. There was macaroni and cheese, green beans, raspberry Jell-O, a milk container and a small paper cup with two mints in it, which she found later to be squares of chewing gum.

Surprisingly, she was hungry. The chicken went down first. While it would never make the menu at one of the finer restaurants in town, it still had a welcome taste to it. Lydia devoured the rest of the meal and swallowed the cold milk in two gulps. Still thirsty, she poured herself a glass of water and drank it all, refilling the glass once more and drinking half of that.

"Getting your strength back?" A male attendant picked up the tray and backed away from the bed. He stumbled into the black nurse but didn't drop the tray. Excusing himself, he slipped past the curtain as the nurse approached with yet another dosage of pain killers.

"I don't want those," Lydia said.

"Oh, honey, you will. Your body has been through a lot. If you don't take your pills you will be hurting like you can't believe."

Lydia opened her mouth and swallowed the pills, washing them down with the other half a glass of water. She rested awhile then called out to see if anyone else was in the room. No answer. She was alone. The attendant returned and removed the screen. It was now late evening and the sun was setting. Still, the light that surrounded her caused her hurt eye to blink and water.

"We can turn off this light," he said as he flipped a switch near the door. The light directly above her bed went dark. "Is that better?"

"Yes, thank you."

The rest of her time in the room went the same until the Athertons showed up next morning for a quick visit. Lady Atherton looked nervous and explained she'd never liked hospitals. Raymond said little, but seemed to be at ease with both the hospital and with Lydia's condition.

"If you need anything, just ask," he said. "The police contacted your automobile insurance agent and I took the liberty of telling the hospital which company covered your medical and life insurance."

Lydia thanked Raymond and smiled her best at Lady Atherton. The visit ended quickly when Doctor Shaner stepped in again. Quick smiles, quick goodbyes, quick departures.

"Let's see what that eye looks like." The doctor pulled away the tape holding the gauze patch over her left eye and reached for a penlight he had clipped inside the pocket of his lab coat. The tiny beam of light played across her face as Lydia felt the first short stab of pain which caused her tear ducts to open.

"Looks good to me. No real damage, no infection. You'll feel an itch, maybe, and you'll have to resist rubbing the eye when you do. An ice cube wrapped in a washcloth and held against the eye will ease the discomfort. Otherwise, give it a few days and you shouldn't have anymore trouble with it. But if you do, just call the appointment desk and they will make arrangements right away. You won't have to wait long."

He left, telling her she could check out whenever she was ready.

She was ready.

Lydia dressed, called her mother, and signed herself out of the hospital when her mother arrived.

"Are you sure you don't want me to stay with you, dear?" her mother asked once they pulled into Lydia's driveway.

"No, mother. Helen can take care of anything I might need. I'm just tired. I'm going to sleep off all the medicine they pumped into me and see how I feel after that. I'd just be poor company for you, I'm afraid."

"Well, if you're sure."

Lydia watched her mother pull out of the drive, relieved that the woman did not insist on staying with her. They didn't get along well anyway, no gross arguing like some families do, just nothing in common. Lydia went inside and straight to bed.

Del Garrett

Chapter 5

WHEN SHE AWOKE at seven the next morning, Lydia went to the bathroom and looked in the mirror. The bright lights of the vanity blinded her at first and sent a stabbing pain into her damaged left eye. The yellow walls were decorated with hundreds of small, pink and white rosebuds. All of them appeared blurred to Lydia. She opened the tap and ran some cold water over her hands which she then rubbed over her face, getting the sleep out of her eyes. She had to lean over the counter, with her face practically touching the mirror, before she got close enough to see the damage to her left eye. Other than it being red and a little swollen, there was only a tiny line in the lower left corner of the eyeball where a miniscule shard of glass had pierced it. Half an inch higher and to the center, she could have suffered partial, if not total blindness.

Satisfied that she didn't look like the *Bride of Frankenstein*, Lydia brushed her hair and applied her makeup. She did this slowly because the catch in her muscles hurt so much she couldn't move as freely as she was used to doing. She only used the bare essentials of makeup today, a little foundation and a little color, because there seemed no need in doing anything more now that Josh was gone. She almost laughed when she thought about it. Everything about her life had centered around her husband, his business, his friends, his demands that she look like a *Barbie Doll* in the flesh. Already, Lydia knew her life had changed; she just didn't know where it would go or what she would do with herself...and right now, she didn't really care. Fixing up her face had taken a lot of energy. She shuffled her way back to bed and collapsed on it. She did not go back to sleep. Wide awake but suffering aches and pains, she managed to get through the morning until Helen looked in on her. Lydia turned down breakfast, calling for chilled orange juice and hot coffee instead.

She crawled out of bed around noon and checked messages on the answering machine. One was from the funeral home where Josh's body had been prepared. *When would she like to consummate the funeral?* "Soon," she told the mechanical voice coming from the speaker. The second message was from Josh's attorney. There would be a reading of the will and disposition of all accounts. The third message was from the Athertons, an invitation to visit them for lunch...to talk. A solemn sound in Raymond's voice. To talk, he'd said. *What was there to talk about?* Did he and Josh have unfinished business, or did the Athertons want to lend her a dry shoulder to cry on? Lydia decided she would take care of the funeral parlor first, the lawyer second, then visit with the Athertons. She called them to let them know it would be later in the day before she could get there.

She selected a black skirt with matching jacket and a dark gray blouse and a pink and white Cameo broach. She pulled a black pillbox hat from the closet. It had a veil and would go well with her mourning clothes. She wondered if she should wear a hat. Satisfied that she didn't need one until the funeral, she put it back in the top of her closet and grabbed her purse. She picked up her keys on the way out to the garage, left a note for the housekeeper to pack Josh's clothes in boxes and to have Lewis, the gardener, set them outside by the garage. She would call the church and have someone come by to pick them up. Somebody, somewhere would put them to good use. She climbed inside her forest green Mini Cooper with white stripes and pulled out of the garage and onto the main drag heading for the funeral parlor, where she arranged for the services to be held on Wednesday, five days since the accident. Today was Monday. That gave enough time to notify her mother, the only relative other than herself who would attend the funeral. Josh had been an orphan. He grew up in Saint Anthony's in Santa Monica until he aged out of the institution. She would call Mother Patricia and tell her when the ceremony would be. Father Michael would want to perform the service.

Lydia called Peter Manning from the Mini Cooper. He could see her within the hour. She dodged the traffic for twelve miles, all the way to the Union Bank Plaza on South Figueroa Street. Manning's office was on the twelfth floor. From any angle, the light gray structure with its rows upon rows of windows rose thirty stories high. Hideous looking building, Lydia thought. Although the Union Bank Plaza had once been a landmark building leading to the development of the business district, it blanched in comparison with the ultra-modern architecture that Josh had created. His eye for aesthetics had been written about in all the trade magazines and had earned him an inside page of *Time Magazine* devoted to on-the-rise entrepreneurs. No more. What he had already built would be his legacy. What had been his vision would be adopted by some other bright and brainy designer. Time for Lydia to move on and forget the parties, the wheeling and dealing, the limelight existence she had shared with her husband. She left the elevator and headed to Manning's office, conscious now that most of the pain had gone away. She moved easier, much like her old self, and only an occasional twitch reminded her that she'd been in a car wreck. She stumbled. Feeling the give in the soft carpet beneath her feet as she walked, she wondered, *Why didn't I wear flats?* She opened the door and was met with the smiling face of Eilene Lockhart, Manning's secretary. Lydia couldn't remember ever talking to Eilene except when she answered the phone and put Lydia through to her boss, never a real conversation. Josh had done all of their legal paperwork.

"Mr. Manning will see you in a moment, Mrs. Taylor. He's with another client right now"

The secretary offered Lydia a cup of coffee but she declined it. Waiting to see her lawyer, she picked up a copy of the Los Angeles Times and briefed through it. She came to a story about the art theft in Paris, the same story that had been on the radio when she and Josh sat at the marina admiring his latest purchase. The L.A. Times reported that authorities in the French capital had egg on their faces and a high-profile mystery on their hands. Lydia didn't finish reading the article because at that moment Manning's secretary knocked on her boss' door and announced Lydia's presence.

"Lydia, please come in." Manning stood up, came around his desk and took Lydia by the hand. "I'm so sorry about Josh. I know how upset you must be. Please sit down. Can I get you anything?"

Eilene had remained by the door. When Lydia shook her head, refusing any refreshment, the secretary quietly withdrew, closing the door behind her.

Manning talked while Lydia listened. She was Josh's only listed relative, therefore, all of his holdings would go to her. His investments were sound and would be transferred at a later time.

"Right now, we need to make sure the bank accounts are completely all in your name, the house, the other real estate—things that involve money and transactions of an immediate nature. Long-term investments we can deal with later."

"Real estate? I wasn't aware Josh owned

anything except our home in Holmby Hills."

Holmby Hills was part of the Golden Triangle, which included Bel Air and Beverly Hills. Josh chose the location because of its stunning view, tucked away along the foothills of a section of the Santa Monica Mountains which also bordered the University of California at Los Angeles and Sunset Boulevard to the south. Lesser known of the triangle developments, perhaps, Holmby Hills had fewer sightseers and its owners were just as well off economically as any of the other residential sections nearby, movie stars mostly, other people in the entertainment business including their neighbor, the late pop star Michael Jackson.

Also, Holmby Hills lies just northwest of the Los Angeles Country Club on Wilshire Boulevard. Business and golf go hand in hand among the affluent and the club offered two eighteen-hole courses plus tennis. Like so much else in Josh's life, Raymond Atherton had been Josh's sponsor. Without Raymond's influence, Josh would not have met the requisite profile preferred by the club's Board of Directors. But club members took eagerly to Josh's wit and charm and his willingness to serve on community projects. In no time, Josh had earned the respect of even the most senior members. Josh made many contacts within the group so he visited the club often, spending more time in the clubhouse than on the courses. Lydia preferred tennis and was glad they lived so close by. She wasn't a good player, but Josh had encouraged her to take lessons from the club's pro, and she enjoyed going there each week.

"Investments only," Manning told her about her husband's other real estate holdings. "All undeveloped properties. I assure you that there's plenty of money in your bank account so that you won't have to sell anything unless you want to. The market is stable. My recommendation is that you take a vacation, find some peace and quiet and deal with your affairs later. I'll need your power of attorney so I can handle things for you the way I did for Josh."

Lydia nodded her head and signed the forms that he presented to her. Eilene notarized them and filed them away, giving Lydia her personal copy. Manning's advice sounded good to Lydia. She didn't want to spend another night in the house without Josh. She stood and said her goodbyes, thanking her lawyer for his help, and headed to her last stop of the day.

Chapter 6

THE ATHERTONS WERE HAPPY TO SEE HER. Happy to see that she looked okay after the accident and that she was keeping her spirits up, as up as could be expected after losing a loved one. Over lunch, they inquired about her finances, did she have enough to take care of her immediate needs, and what could they do to help her. That opened the question about staying in the empty house.

"Oh, my dear, why don't you stay with us for awhile?" Lady Atherton held Lydia's hands and comforted her.

"Thank you. You've both been very kind to me and I appreciate it, but if I'm going to be alone now, I need to get used to that. I'll find a place and spend some time getting used to the idea of being on my own."

"Maybe we can still help," Raymond said. "We have a small villa in Carmel. It's just sitting there unused. An old couple tends to the place for us, Vito and Sophia Fanucci. You'll like them. The neighbors like their privacy so they won't be too nosy. You'll find it quiet and to your liking. Please take it for the summer, or for however long you need it."

Lydia thought about their offer for a moment. She wanted to get away from L.A. and it didn't matter where. "You're so kind. Yes, I'll accept. Carmel sounds like just the right place for me to get away to. I'll go home and pack and make the trip tonight."

"Fine," Raymond said. "I'll call the Fanuccis and tell them to expect you." Raymond wrote down the directions and telephone number in case she couldn't find the place. Lydia thanked him and left.

She hurried home and packed. Carmel was a six-hour trip, depending on the traffic and how fast one drives. Lydia took time to relax and swallow an energy drink. She called her housekeeper, Helen, and gave her two day's off with pay. She could afford to be generous, considering that she was planning on selling the house and the housekeeper and gardener would probably be out of a job soon unless she bought another place close by. She didn't call the gardener, though. She reasoned that if she were to sell the place it would have to look well groomed. She would give each of them a nice bonus when she moved away.

Lydia stopped at a service station before leaving L.A. and filled the Mini Cooper with gas, then took the scenic Pacific Coast Highway north through San Luis Obispo to Big Sur, then twenty-six miles further on to Carmel, arriving at nine o'clock that night. She could have saved some time by taking Interstate 5 then connecting to Highway 101, but she preferred the view along the coast—something she shared with Josh—and, besides, she wasn't in any hurry.

The Fanuccis had stayed up and greeted her

as if they already knew her. Sophia was a jolly fat woman with big, dark eyes and hair still dark although she must have been in her late sixties. She wore her hair in a bun looking very much like she belonged in an Italian movie.

Vito, who looked older, was a thin man with leathery brown skin and close-cropped gray hair. He had small slits for eyes and thick glasses like twin magnifiers, and a pencil thin mustache. He carried Lydia's bags to her room while Sophia ushered her into the kitchen and insisted that she eat a bowl of minestrone.

Lydia smelled the flavorful soup and took a spoonful. Invigorating. She ate half the bowl before she stopped and told Sophia how good it tasted. The woman smiled and shoved a plate of freshly baked garlic bread toward her. Lydia didn't eat bread in quantities, but like the soup its flavor was too much to resist. When she had finished the bowl,

Sophia removed the plates and handed Lydia a cup of steaming fresh tea. During it all, Sophia had talked non-stop about how happy she was to have another female in the house, that Vito was such poor company, that she was sure Lydia would enjoy her stay. When Lydia yawned, Sophia excused herself for talking so much. She showed Lydia the way to the master bedroom.

"We will talk more in the morning," she told the new lady of the house.

"Thank you so much," Lydia replied. "I guess all the activity of the day is finally catching up to me."

"Sleep well." Sophia waddled out of the room and Lydia kicked off her shoes. She lay back on the bed and closed her eyes for a moment. She awoke half an hour later, bemused that she had fallen asleep while still dressed. She removed the rest of her clothes and selected a light blue nightgown from her suitcase. She would put her things away tomorrow. She was too tired to bother with them tonight.

Chapter 7

A KNOCK ON THE DOOR brought Lydia out of a sound sleep. Sophia entered with a breakfast tray in her hand and waited for Lydia to prop herself up before setting it in her lap. The tray held covered silver dishes of food and a small white vase with a single red rose in it. Sophia placed the tray across Lydia's lap and moved to the window to open the curtains and let the morning sunlight flood the room. The rays of light played across the maroon and crème lace bedspread and pillow shams, which gave a regal look to the simple country style bed. Lydia felt the warmth of the sunlight as it touched her face, adding to the glow already there from the full night of sleep she'd had. She also noticed that the sunlight no longer hurt her eyes. She smiled and enjoyed even more the feeling of waking up without a care in the world. Sophia smiled back at her, thinking the expression on Lydia's face had something to do with her presence.

A variety of artwork covered the walls, overcrowding the room with painted flowers, mountain views and Napoleonic scenes of Paris, its streets filled with people strolling along amid shops and restaurants, and with an occasional portrait of children at play, each painting a tribute to the artist's command of the light which centered on the main subjects and left the rest of the canvas in subdued ambiance.

"You're going to spoil me with all this delicious food," Lydia said. She uncovered the tray and caught the first whiff of scrambled eggs and Canadian bacon. Wheat toast and a spoon of strawberry jam sat on an adjacent saucer, coffee and orange juice completed the meal.

"I didn't know if you took cream or sugar with your coffee."

"Yes, both. I have to sweeten it or I can't stand the stuff."

"Don't ever let Vito make coffee for you." Sophia laughed and wrinkled her nose. "He uses too many grounds, it comes out of the pot like mud." Sophia threw up her hands to show her disgust. "He is no cook, either. He burns his bacon, likes his eggs runny, and uses half a jar of jam on his toast. Terrible, terrible man, but I love him so much."

"That's why he has you." Lydia smiled. "You seem like you were made for each other."

Sophia sighed. "Forty-two years we've been married. *Oy*. What I put up with being married to that man."

Lydia liked this woman. It was plain to see that the Fanuccis might be set in their ways, but they were comfortable with each other, and as much in love as they must have been when they first married. No couple could be as opposite as these two and remain married so long.

"Yes, he knows he got a prize when he married me." Sophia leaned closer to Lydia and lowered her voice in a conspiratorial tone, "And I never let him forget that."

Lydia laughed so hard she nearly spilled her coffee.

Sophia excused herself, letting Lydia enjoy her breakfast alone. Before leaving, she placed that morning's newspaper beside the breakfast tray and patted Lydia on the arm.

"Enjoy. I'll be back in a few minutes to pick up the tray."

Lydia was surprisingly famished. The eggs and bacon went down rapidly and she settled back with a slice of toast and jam and sipped her coffee while she looked at the newspaper. She wasn't interested in the news, or sports. The comics gave her a laugh or two, always nice to start the day in a good mood. She settled on the community pages, seeing which restaurants looked appealing and what entertainment was being offered.

Her search landed on an ad for the Mission Carmel Basilica on Rio Road where an all-girl choir was performing a series of concerts of Renaissance and Baroque music from New Spain to benefit the California missions. Interesting, she thought, but not for today. Lydia had been to Carmel before and knew it offered some of the best shopping in the state.

The city is small with a narrow main street lined by art galleries and bakeries. She remembered the way the bakeries smelled during her last visit, fresh breads and sweet rolls with flavored icings that tantalized the tongue, and fruit cups with freshly diced peaches, pears and strawberries chilled lightly and generously scooped on top of warm apple cinnamon cakes fresh from the oven. She also remembered that Carmel has a nice beach, which she now saw in the pictures in the newspaper. A day at the beach listening to the surf wash up on the sand sounded like a pleasant way to rid herself of all her troubles, at least for a while.

Lydia threw down the paper and jumped out of bed, eager to find her swim suit. She had brought two of them with her, a full turquoise Catalina swim suit and a blue and white polka dot bikini, which she chose, wearing it under an open blue jacket that came to mid-thigh. Some people might frown upon a new widow dressing so boldly and enjoying herself in the California sun, but she wasn't the least bit concerned. She loved Josh, and missed him dearly and that was that. But the practical side of her—that part of her personality that told her she'd just survived a car crash and that life was too short to mourn forever—gave her to believe that she should immediately get on with her life. Their lawyer had suggested that, so had the Athertons. And nobody in Carmel seeing her in her bikini would know that she was so recently widowed. She'd return for Josh's funeral and wear her widow's weeds, but life was too short and she was too young to spend her time in everlasting sorrow. She knew that she should feel the sorrow, and she should feel guilty at not doing so, but people mourn in their own way, she acknowledged. All she wanted right now was to get away from everything for a couple days and clear her mind so she could deal with whatever she'd need to when she got back home to Los Angeles; then, after the funeral, she would return to Carmel and let the sea call her name each day and night until she felt whole again.

She drove around the city leisurely taking in the sights it offered. She watched the tourists stopping to look in windows at whatever was on display. Clothing stores offered brightly colored casual attire for the beach, other stores offered souvenirs, trinkets, and exotic pets of all kinds—parrots, hamsters, snakes. After a few hours, as dusk fell on the resort area, Lydia stopped at a sidewalk café for a bite to eat and a glass of wine.

Sitting at the next table, a chatty broad in yellow-flowered Capri pants and a white cotton shirt tied at the waist with all three top buttons undone, displayed her ample cleavage under a hot pink stretch top that showed she wasn't wearing a bra underneath the thin material. The woman had bobbed cut red hair with short shanks of it flying all over the place in the wind. She held her hair in place rather vainly by a yellow scarf tied behind her neck. Huge, crescent-moon earrings swung back and forth as she turned her head to talk non-stop to other women sitting on either side of her.

Lydia hadn't intended to snoop, but the woman talked so loud and dirty about her latest 'boyfriend' that Lydia couldn't help but listen.

"He likes to use toys on me," she told her dinner companions. "Truth is, he likes me to use them on him. He's more of a slut than I am."

"Well, that takes a lot of doing," one of the other women said, placing the back of her hand across her mouth as if she were trying to whisper it, but making sure everyone at the tables nearest them heard what she had to say.

"Well, screw you, dear heart. I happen to know you get down and dirty once in awhile, yourself."

"Only when I'm with somebody or by myself." They all three laughed, as did Lydia.

A young man at the next table plucked out a Spanish sounding tune on a classical guitar. The notes captured Lydia's attention. She liked the way he was dressed. He wore khaki colored cargo shorts and a blue denim shirt with the sleeves rolled up over his biceps. An abundance of pockets covered both his cargo shorts and the shirt he wore, including the top of its sleeves. His sandy hair hung loosely over the left side of his face. He wore walking shoes without socks and tapped his right foot in rhythm to the music he played. Lydia found him attractive and immediately chastised herself for thinking so. *What's wrong with me?* She could justify being carefree in an attempt to relax, but taking notice of another man in that way was not a proper way for a widow to act, even in California. Still, there was something about him that attracted her. Lydia couldn't help but listen to his music and smile at the lovely way he played while tapping her toes to the Spanish rhythm.

Chapter 8

"He's quite good, isn't he?" It took Lydia a moment to realize the red haired woman was talking to her.

"*Huh?* Oh, yes. He plays very well."

"He does that, my dear. Very well indeed." The sexual inference was obvious. Lydia felt a warmth rise up around her neck. The red head smiled lasciviously and ran her tongue along her upper lip. Lydia blushed but kept silent and listened to the young man finish his song.

"Hi, I'm Marge." The red head scooted out of her chair and plopped herself down in one of the chairs at Lydia's table. She landed a huge shopping bag in her lap, holding it with one hand and holding a glass of white wine with the other.

Lydia hadn't noticed that the woman's two friends had left. *She's looking for an audience,* Lydia thought, *and I'm the only other person around.*

Marge motioned for the young man to join them. She introduced him to Lydia as Mitch, an old high school chum. He propped his guitar up in one of the vacant chairs at the table and slouched his body into the other, draping a tanned leg over the arm of the chair and smiling at Lydia.

"Will you marry me?" His joke took Lydia by surprise. She blushed and laughed.

"Ignore him," Marge said, "He proposes to all the cute girls he sees. Say, I haven't seen you around here before."

"I'm just here for a couple of days, had to get out of L.A. for a while."

"Oh, I can't blame you there, honey. Why would you ever want to live in L.A. with all the gangs and traffic congestion and those absurd actors? They're all so unreasonably caught up in themselves, so...*incongruous*." Marge held onto the last word as if it had been scripted for her by some screenwriter. She gestured with an open hand and shook her wispy hair free of the yellow scarf and laughed loudly.

Lydia almost said it was where she and her husband lived and worked, then caught herself. She had no husband. Not anymore. For that matter, she had no job either.

"You're right, it's a filthy place; I just sort of wound up there. Some friends of mine own a place here and they've let me use it."

"Good for them. Mitch, quit staring holes in her blouse."

Mitch's smile widened and he looked directly at Lydia's bikini top. Lydia looked down, embarrassed, but to her relief nothing was showing, certainly not showing as much as was Marge's outfit. Still, she pulled her jacket closed and fastened one of the large white buttons on it, which caused the young man to throw his head back and laugh at her shyness.

"I said, stop staring. You can stare at my tits if you wish." Marge popped out her chest and pulled back her shirt so her breasts were totally visible under the pink top.

"I've seen your tits," Mitch said. "I haven't seen this lady's."

"Well, at least he called you a lady. He never does that for me."

"That's because you're a slut. It's just a good thing for you that I like sluts."

Marge flashed him a finger. "Sit on this and rotate, you bastard." She was laughing. "Don't you think we're just awful?" she said to Lydia.

"I don't know what to think," Lydia said bemused at their banter.

The three of them chatted back and forth for a few more minutes. The shock of their language wore away and Lydia found she actually enjoyed the conversation. It was nice to talk to someone about things other than wheeling and dealing or about funeral arrangements or bank accounts. After awhile, though, she excused herself and said she had to go. Marge asked if Lydia would mind giving Mitch a ride since she was heading in the opposite direction and Mitch's car was in the shop. Not wanting to, but not knowing how to say no politely, she reluctantly agreed.

"I'm just going down the road a few miles to see some guys I know at a club. We get together when we can, drink a few beers and play music. Want to come?"

Lydia begged off on the club, saying maybe another time. After she dropped him there, she drove back toward the villa.

She stopped for gas on her way and, although

darkness had fallen, she walked across the highway to look at the silvery foam of the ocean splashing against a dark outcropping of rocks. The waves broke hard as they struck the formation, sending spirals of foamy white spray rushing skyward like a geyser. They crashed down heavily on the green fungi covered stones in loud smashing, thundering sounds. There was something mesmerizing in their sound and fury as they slapped the stones and softly blended back with the dark ocean water again before rejoining the tide in its slow and easy wash upon the beach. This was the primordial beginning of life on the planet, Lydia thought. She remembered that from her science classes in high school. How much more fun high school would have been if the teachers had taken the students out of the classrooms and took them out into the real world and taught them firsthand knowledge instead of what was merely written in the textbooks.

Lydia sensed another person close to her. The other person turned out to be Frank Davis, the waiter from the restaurant. He was also admiring the view.

"Hello, hello," he said, approaching Lydia. His voice had an Australian accent. "Didn't I see you just up the road a bit?"

"At the restaurant, yes. You work there?"

He nodded.

"I just got off shift and came here to grab some petrol for my car. I see you did the same thing," he said, pointing toward the Mini Cooper.

"I like those cars. Cute, and good gas mileage. Did you see *The Italian Job?* It's about a bank heist and the robbers use Mini Coopers for getaway cars."

"Yes, I saw the movie; both of them, really. The one with Mark Wahlberg was good, but so was the original one with Michael Cain."

"Oh, a regular movie buff, are you? That's great. I like the movies, too."

They talked some more. Frank was twenty-eight, same as Josh had been. He was from Boroloola in the Northern Territory off the Gulf of Carpentaria, which is why he loved the ocean so much, he told her, it reminded him of home. He said he was an art major who had left home because his father persecuted him for not following in the family fishing business. He had promised himself he would strike it rich in California. "So far, that hasn't happened, I'm afraid." He laughed. "Fact is, I've just been booted out of my flat. I'm sleeping in my Volkswagon tonight."

Lydia felt sorry for Frank, knowing that her sense of being lost wasn't exactly the same as his, but he seemed kind and needed a place to stay. Without thinking things through, she asked if he'd like to spend the night at the villa.

"Sure I wouldn't be putting you out, none?"

"No, I—I'm sure it will be all right." She was wondering what Vito and Sophia might think, or the Athertons if they told them. *What the hell*, she thought. *I've already asked him and he's accepted.* She could tell from the smile on his face that he was relieved he wouldn't be sleeping in his car tonight.

Frank followed Lydia until they got to the villa. He parked behind her in the driveway. Vito and Sophia had gone to spend some time with friends. Sophia had left a note for Lydia saying this was their canasta night and they would be out until very late.

Lydia offered to fix Frank a sandwich but he said he had already grabbed something at the restaurant. Instead, they sat in the kitchen drinking wine and talking. Hours went by and Lydia arose, telling him there was a room over the garage that he could use.

Frank grabbed a bag from his car and followed her across the driveway and up the stairs leading to the room. Lydia hadn't actually been inside, but she had looked through the window earlier that morning and Sophia had told her it was for guests.

The door was unlocked. Nobody locked their doors in Carmel. The city has a violent crime rate of only 207 incidents per 100,000 people, less than half of California's rate of 511 and 676 nation-wide. Once inside the room, Lydia checked the bed and found it had fresh sheets on it. The refrigerator had cold beverages and the cabinet beside it had canned snacks.

"Looks like you'll be okay for the night."

"Thanks. I won't need anything but some water to drink and some to splash on my body to get clean."

"Well, if you do need anything, come to the house and ask."

Frank moved toward Lydia, wrapped an arm around her waist and pulled her to him. He started to kiss her but Lydia put a hand on his chest stopping him. It was too soon. She felt comfortable talking to him, but she was a grieving widow even if she didn't show it. Of course, Frank didn't know that so he acted like any red-blooded young male alone in a room with a beautiful woman dressed in a bikini.

"*Uh*—I didn't invite you here for that," Lydia stuttered.

"Sorry," he said, releasing his hold on her. "I didn't mean to be ungentlemanly."

"I'm coming out of some…difficulties; I'm just not ready for anything like that."

"It's okay," he said and backed away from her. "Maybe some other time when you're ready."

Lydia bid him goodnight and left. She thought about leaving a note for Sophia, but decided it wasn't necessary. She'd had a full day and night and wanted to get to bed. But she couldn't sleep. She stayed awake trying to read a book but couldn't concentrate on the story in it.

She felt that empty feeling deep inside of her that she always felt when Josh was gone away on business. But he wouldn't be coming home this time and that made her sorrow even deeper. She still felt Frank's arms around her and it felt good even though it shouldn't. He wasn't Josh. *It's just my nerves*, she thought. She knew she was still in shock over losing her husband even though she was in full control outwardly. *What am I doing here?* She couldn't run away from what was inside of her. Here or in Los Angeles, she would still have that emptiness inside.

"Why would you ever want to live in L.A.?"

Lydia thought about it. L.A.'s fine most of the time for business, but she didn't want to live there anymore.

She liked what she had seen here in Carmel. Maybe this was the place where she should settle down. She yawned. Sleep had finally crept upon her and Lydia welcomed it.

She dropped the book she'd been reading and lay her head back on the pillow. She fell asleep instantly and dreamed of Josh and the smell of the ocean and having fun with him on the yacht they never got to sail. No thoughts of the accident until early morning when she awoke at the sound of the curtains being opened and the sunlight flooding in again, which in her half-asleep state reminded her of the car's lights coming on at the accident scene. She threw up her hands instinctively and Sophia looked worried for her.

Briefly, Lydia recalled seeing Josh's head dangling upside down and then Lydia came fully awake and the vision was gone.

Chapter 9

THE SMALL MOTORBOAT ROSE AND FELL over the waves as Pietro steered its bow toward the light on the other shore, the Dungeness Lighthouse at the southernmost point of Kent would provide him with a quieter shoreline than most of the area south of Dover. Also, it was without prying eyes to see him land. Dungeness Lighthouse was converted to automatic operation in 1991 and is monitored and controlled from the Trinity House Operations and Planning Centre at Harwich.

Pietro had wrapped the rolled up paintings in a second oil cloth before leaving the marina in Boulogne, France, to protect them from the salty sea spray covering everything on deck, and draped a tarpaulin over them for added protection. He had lowered his hood because there was no longer a need to wear it up and now felt the freshness of the sea spray upon his face. He smiled and tasted the salt from the sea in his mouth. Above him, only the Morning Star still shined. A faint gray haze covered the water and Pietro heard three blasts of the fog horn which sounded every minute, but he could now see the land and the black and white striped lighthouse, and powered down his small craft so he could look out for the rocks that jutted dangerously along the shore line. When the first rock came into view, Pietro killed the engine entirely. The rocks were covered in green algae. Slick to the touch, no doubt, he used an oar to skirt around each rock. When he drifted past the final black stone, he used the oar to paddle his way the remaining hundred yards to the beach.

Pietro pulled the boat onto dry land and sank the anchor into the sand, shoving it in deep with the sole of his combat boot. He retrieved the six rolls of canvasses from under the tarp and jerked upright as he heard footsteps coming up behind him.

"Is that you?" A raspy voice whispered behind him and Pietro whirled around with the stolen art in one hand and a small pistol in the other.

"Hey, mate. Take it easy. It's me, Edward."

"Sorry, Craven. Have to be careful, you know."

Edward Craven hobbled up to Pietro and pointed a finger at the rolls under Pietro's arm.

"You got a good haul, did you?"

"Yes. A good haul. I got everything I went after."

"And I'll bet them *froggies* are still crapping their pants with you in and out like you were."

Pietro smiled.

"Let's get out of here. You have a car?"

"Up the bank. Just leave everything here and I'll come back up after lunch. No one'll bother it."

"No matter if they do. There's nothing in it worth stealing." Pietro smiled and tapped the six rolls of art under his arm with the barrel of his pistol as if to say he had the only things that mattered. He stuffed the short barrel of the Walther PPS into his pocket and headed up the bank to where Craven had indicated the car would be.

Craven, assisted by a walking stick, climbed the bank with some difficulty. When he reached the car, a 1966 English Ford Anglia, he unlocked his door and climbed inside, reaching across to unlock the other door for Pietro.

"Say, Petey. Where'd you want to go, anyway?"

"I'll be staying the night at Lydd on Sea and you can pick me up tomorrow. I'll fly out of Lydd Airport."

"Why bother staying at all?"

"Because I'm tired. I'm hungry. I need some cigarettes and I want to get laid. Any objections?"

Craven shook his head, laughed, and started the car. Pietro catnapped all the way to Lydd on Sea and said nothing as he got out of the car. He nodded a goodbye to Craven.

"What time does your plane leave tomorrow?" Craven had rolled down his window and shouted at Pietro. Raindrops fell as they spoke.

"I have to check in at four o'clock."

"Right, then. I'll pick you up in plenty of time, mate."

Craven hurriedly rolled up his window and drove away. Pietro entered the small office where he picked up a key. He'd rented the room by mail in advance. The cute blonde lady behind the counter smiled at him as she gave the key to him. He asked when she got off duty and she answered. The timing was good for him. He would be hungry by the time she got off duty. Hungry for a good meal and hungry for other things. The first thing he wanted to do was take a shower and get some sleep. He did that, waking up shortly before four o'clock. The blonde was due to end her shift at five. That gave him plenty of time to freshen up and get ready for an interesting evening. He wanted to call his parents to let them know everything was okay but didn't want to leave behind any kind of trail the police could follow. He would wait until he got back to Canada and call them from there.

Chapter 10

"GOOD MORNING, SLEEPYHEAD." Sophia sat a breakfast tray on Lydia's lap and sat herself on the bed beside Lydia. "Got anything you want to tell me?"

"Huh? Oh, we have a house guest."

Lydia told the housekeeper about meeting Frank and that he had no place to stay. She assured Sophia that all she wanted to do was to help out another human being down on his luck.

"I think it is a good thing you do," Sophia reassured her. "I will take him a bite to eat and a strong cup of coffee."

"Thank you, Sophia. I promise he won't stay long."

Frank was already up when Sophia knocked on the door to the guest house. He charmed her with his smile and followed her to the kitchen in the main house to eat his sausage and egg biscuit she'd prepared for him and to finish his second cup of coffee. He'd already made coffee in the guest house and emptied his first cup before Sophia arrived. She happily refilled his cup from the pot on the counter and poured herself one while they talked.

"She doesn't know much about you," Sophia said.

"No, and I prefer it that way," Frank replied.

"She's a nice girl. I don't want to see her get hurt more than she already has been."

"I don't either. She's vulnerable right now. I know that, but it's not her emotions that I want to tamper with."

"She is quite rich."

"Money's only good when you don't have it."

"The money, she won't miss. But if you hurt her...."

"Wouldn't dream of it. You know me. I'm just out for a buck."

"I should think the Athertons pay you well enough for the art you provide."

"There's never enough money. I spend everything I make."

Lydia, by this time, had gotten dressed and came down the stairs with her breakfast tray. She hadn't heard the conversation between Frank and Sophia. She bid Frank a cheery good morning.

"I told this very nice lady," he pointed his coffee cup toward Sophia, "that I got up this morning, called a friend from UCLA who's offered to put me up. I also called an agent I'd left some of my paintings with and she says she has a buyer for one and asked if I had enough for a showing. Looks like my luck is about to change."

"Where—when will you go?"

"Oh, my friend lives just the other side of Big Sur from here. It's the perfect inspiration for my portraits of the sea. I will give up my job at the restaurant. The sale from the paintings will carry me over until the showing. With any luck, I'll make enough after her commission to continue on."

They talked more about Frank's plans. When he was all packed, he asked when he could see her again. Lydia explained that she had to take care of some business but would be back in Carmel in a few days.

"Nice young man," Sophia said as they watched Frank pull out of the driveway. "You should see him again."

"Oh, no. I don't think so. It's too soon. It's not proper."

"What's proper these days? You loved your husband. But now you are alone. It's no good to be alone."

"People would think badly of me."

"What people? You said you had no really close friends, except the Athertons and I'm sure they wouldn't think badly of you. They like you very much."

"It's true, I don't have a lot of close friends. Most of my acquaintances were Josh's business friends."

"And you won't see them anymore."

"No, I won't. Just our lawyer. Still, I need a little more time before I'm ready to see anyone on a social level."

"Go home, bury your husband; come back here when you're done and start living again."

Lydia smiled. She felt like she had found a big sister who was giving her sound advice. Losing Josh had been devastating, especially in such a horrible way, Car crashes don't just hurt the ones who die, they hurt the ones who live.

Lydia loaded the Mini Cooper for her return trip to Los Angeles. She would take care of her obligations, both as widow and as new owner of the estate. She was glad that Peter Manning was looking after things for her. She had already decided to sell the house and move to Carmel. She could have joined her mother in San Francisco but she preferred being on her own rather than having her mother tell her what to do. That's one of the reasons she'd married Josh. Her mother was a wonderful person. She knew that, and everyone who knew her mother told her that; but mothers can be stifling sometimes and hers usually was most of the time.

Lydia accepted the fact that she didn't have it all together, especially now with Josh gone, but she didn't need her mother overly doting on her from one minute to the next, making decisions for her. *I'll get by on my own. What I don't know about life, I'll learn.* She perked herself up, said goodbye to the Fanuccis and headed back to Los Angeles along the Pacific Coast Highway. She pulled into her own driveway that afternoon a few minutes past two. She checked her mail, checked her answering machine—one call from her mother, another from Manning, and one from some local politician wanting her to vote for him.

She unpacked, selected her suit for tomorrow's funeral, complete with the black hat and veil, and a sensible set of black wedged shoes. She could walk in heels, but why take the chance of stumbling at the gravesite? *I'm such a klutz.* She made a supper of cold beef, left over rice pilaf and half a peach, turned on Oprah and kicked back to rest.

Her mother called again.

"Mom, I'm fine. Quit worrying about me. I spent the night in Carmel just to get away for awhile. I'm okay. I'll see you at the funeral tomorrow."

"I'll be there for you, darling. *Uh*—I'm bringing Teddy with me, if that's all right."

Teddy was, politely speaking, her mother's new companion. He was much younger than her mother and quite handsome. Lydia didn't care that much for him, not to say she disliked him any, more that she was neutral about him. She just didn't care. If anything, she was glad to see the smile on her mother's face, knowing that Teddy put it there didn't matter.

"It's fine, mother. Bring your 'toy boy' with you."

"Oh, how cruel. Teddy is such a comfort to me. You'll see, being alone is no fun."

Lydia laughed at the thought. Her mother had never been truly alone. After Lydia's father died, her mother started dating right away, the first man she dated turned out to be the son of the funeral director. If Lydia had any reason not to feel guilty about enjoying Frank's company last night, it was because her mother was such a good role model.

"No problem, mother. I'm sure you'll feel much better having someone come along with you."

"Well, to do the driving if no other reason."

Helen showed up early the next morning. She went about her business, preparing for guests that evening after the funeral. Lydia came down the stairs in her widow's weeds and greeted her. She okayed Helen's selection for a buffet of cold cuts, potato salad, fruit and snack trays. Funerals always make people hungry. Lydia looked outside at the dark clouds rolling in. Yes, it always rains at funerals. When time came, she joined her mother who had just arrived, and Teddy drove them to the funeral parlor.

Several people attending the service said nice things about Josh. Father Michael arrived from Santa Monica and talked about Josh as a little boy and what a fine man and loving husband he had become, and what a shame it was that his life ended so soon after becoming so successful, "But God always knows best," he concluded.

A few others rose to speak about their relationships with Josh and how nice he had been to them, meaning they made money off his ideas. Finally, Raymond Atherton took center stage and praised Josh for all he had done and for their loving friendship. When he broke down and cried at the end, Lydia wondered if Josh had told her the whole truth about Raymond, that he was homosexual and maybe their friendship had been more than just friendship. But that didn't matter, now. Josh was gone. Besides, she liked Raymond and Lady Atherton for her own reasons. No reason to think badly of them after how nice they had been to her.

The drive to Westwood Village Memorial Park Cemetery on Glendon Avenue seemed to Lydia to take forever. Josh had selected Westwood as their final resting place because he was a fan of the old television show, *Hogan's Heroes,* which starred Bob Crane. The murdered actor was buried across the path from where Josh had purchased a double plot for himself and Lydia. Westwood was also the final resting place for such fine actors as Jack Lemon and Walter Mathieu. Marilyn Monroe was also buried there along with a host of other famous actors, writers and directors. Josh had always enjoyed being seen with Hollywood's finest. It was fitting that he should be buried with some of them.

The rain started slowly, as if in rhythm to the patter of the pallbearers' feet. The six men who carried her husband's coffin were familiar only by their faces. Lydia had met them at various parties and such, but did not know them well enough to say who they were or what their interests might be, job-wise or personal. A large crowd had shown up so Josh must have been well-liked. *Who are these people? I feel like the stranger here.* Lydia took her place on the front row, joined by her mother and Father Michael. The Athertons took seats on the second row but Lydia ushered them to the front. If anyone deserved to share the front row with the family it was this kindly couple.

While the Angels Slept

Again, Father Michael spoke highly of Josh and how the good always have a place in Heaven. He spoke briefly while the attendees huddled close together under a tent, pressing forward against those in chairs, shielding themselves the best they could from the rain.

The rain. Lydia had always liked the rain.

She was grateful for what drops of water she felt sprinkle her face as she lifted her veil and kissed Josh's coffin. She lingered over the polished oak box and came away with her face heavily dampened. She wasn't sure that she had cried any tears. She had sobbed a time or two as Father Michael spoke, but not heavily, not like a widow was supposed to cry over her husband. Knowing how much stock Josh had put in appearances, she was happy the rain had dotted her face, giving her the proper look of someone grieving. *I'm sorry, Josh.* She love him. She knew he'd loved her. Theirs may not have been a conventional love story, but it had suited both of them.

Now it was over. Lydia stepped away from the tent, guided by Father Michael with her mother and Teddy walking behind her. As the crowd stepped aside to let her pass, Lydia's foot slipped out from under her. Father Michael held tightly to one arm while a hand from the crowd reached out to steady her other arm. Lydia looked up to thank the man who had caught her.

Frank Davis looked into Lydia's face as he helped her right herself. *How did he know about the funeral?* Frank held her as Lydia regained her balance. Dark clouds above them darkened his features and added to the look of despair on his face. It was a look Lydia had never seen on him, almost as if he were as lost as she felt. Lydia pulled back from Frank as Father Michael moved her ahead toward the line of cars. She glanced back over her shoulder but Frank had gone, disappeared into the crowd. She rode with Teddy and her mother, leaving the limousine to return to the funeral home.

Back home, Lydia excused herself to the bedroom. She needed a moment alone, not that her mother would allow that. She sat beside Lydia and did her best to comfort her daughter. She said all the words a mother was supposed to say but Lydia paid no attention. Her mind locked on the one thought, Frank Davis. She knew she hadn't told him about Josh or the funeral. Seeing him there did not comfort her. This part of her life had nothing to do with those she met in Carmel. She didn't like mixing the two. Maybe she shouldn't move there after all, no matter how nice and peaceful it was. Where she went next, she wanted it to be a new start without any past. It wasn't as if she had anything to hide, it was simply that she had to find herself. *Who am I, really?* She had been her mother's daughter and Josh's wife, now she had to find who she was for herself. She needed a purpose in life. Right now she needed some rest.

But she didn't do that. *No rest for the weary.*

She composed herself and announced to her mother that she must go downstairs and thank everyone for showing up.

She descended the stairs, looking at each one's face, not seeing the face of the man she'd hoped to see. Raymond met her at the foot of the stairs and took her arm. Lydia smiled politely and greeted each of her guests. Peter Manning stepped forward and whispered that she should come by the office tomorrow. "Anytime you wish. I have the entire day open."

Lydia ended the circle of faces and thanked each of them for coming. Plastic plates piled up on the end of the buffet table and the housekeeper and cook swished them away to a garbage sack in the kitchen. The crowd thinned and finally cleared. Father Michael bid his farewells and bade Lydia to call upon him anytime she felt the need. Teddy kissed her discretely on the cheek and stepped outside to smoke a cigarette, leaving her mother to say goodbye.

"Lydia, I do wish you'd come stay with me for awhile."

"No need, mother. I have a place to stay. I'm going to sell this house as soon as I find a place and get the furniture moved."

"Well, I'm sure you know what's best. I'll call you." Her mother left with Teddy supporting the woman all the way to the car.

The Athertons were the last to leave.

"Thank you so much for letting me use your villa."

"Stay as long as you wish, my dear," Raymond said while Lady Atherton held Lydia by the arm and smiled motherly at her.

"I will, but it won't be long."

The old couple left and Lydia made her way to Helen and thanked her.

"What will you do now?" Helen asked.

"You mean, where will I live?"

"Sorry, ma'am; I hate to be...."

"Don't be sorry. This mess concerns you, too, and the gardener. I've decided to sell the house, but I'll let you know when. Meanwhile, you still have your position here and if I stay in the area, I'll want you with me, of course. But if I move elsewhere, you'll both get my best recommendations and a nice bonus."

"Thank you. Whatever we can do for you, please just ask."

"Well, you can find something to do with all these leftovers. Take what you wish and give the rest to the local shelter. And find me today's newspaper."

There would be no notice yet of Frank's art showing, but Lydia checked the ads anyway, looking for studios. She had no idea which one he'd use, but tomorrow she'd make the rounds and see if she could find him, or find the agent who had called him.

Chapter 11

L YDIA AWOKE EARLY. Splashing cold water on her face she quickly brushed her hair and dressed for the day. She repacked the Mini Cooper and headed towards Big Sur. The sky was bright blue with no clouds to speak of. Traffic was light this early in the morning so she drove with a carefree feeling, letting her hands rest on the steering wheel instead of gripping it. She planned to stop at every tourist spot that looked like it might have a decent café or exhibition, any place where Frank might have hung one of his sketches. There weren't that many.

One of the major attractions about Big Sur is its many miles of under development. Wary travelers, especially those familiar with this stretch of highway, always gassed up before making the trip. In her eagerness, Lydia forgot that. Fortunately, the Mini Cooper was no gas hog. She had stopped twice, once for breakfast at one spot, for coffee at another, and now she pulled in to a small spot that offered fruit and granola with frozen orange juice and imported coffees.

She shopped around the souvenir section and made small talk with the guy behind the cash register. She paid for an orange blast and was about to leave when she noticed a painting hanging behind the register. It was an oil sketch of the seashore under a dark and ominous sky above and a stretch of desolate beach below. A lone figure stood on the beach, looking at the sea waves which crashed against the sparkling sand, appearing lost in his thoughts. Lydia couldn't make out the artist's name.

"I'm interested in your painting."

"That? Some guy stopped by here yesterday and didn't have the price of a meal on him. He offered the painting from a batch he had in a sketch book. It's Big Sur, baby, in all its fury, or so he said. He said he was an art student from Australia. You meet all kinds of folks along this stretch."

"His name is Frank."

"Yeah, I think so. You know him?"

"I may have met him last night."

"Well, tell him no more paintings for meals. I can't stay in business if I don't get cold, hard cash."

"How much was his meal?"

"Came to six bucks, give or take."

"I'll give you double that for the painting."

"Well...."

Realizing he had maybe hooked a fish, the guy held out until Lydia said, "Twenty bucks, take it or leave it."

He took the money and Lydia left with the painting.

More stops along the way proved useless. Lydia gave up and headed to the villa in Carmel. It was still light when she arrived and parked the Mini Cooper in front of the garage. Vito met her as she unloaded her bags.

"Need any help with those?" he asked.

"No thanks. I've got them. I'll be back in a moment to put the car away."

"*Hmmm,* it needs washing. Leave me the keys and I'll put it away when I'm done. I'll bring the keys to you."

"Oh, you're such a dear man." She handed him her key ring and toted her bags inside the house and up the stairs.

"You're back," Sophia said. "I'm so glad. Can I fix you something to eat?"

"No thank you, Sophia. I'm fine, just wanted to get my clothes to my room."

"Well, if you need anything, let me know. Oh, by the way, you got a telephone call."

Sophia waddled her way over to the wall phone in the kitchen where she had stuck a note on the bulletin board. She handed it to Lydia who thanked her and looked at the note. Frank's name was scribbled on it above a number. "It was that nice young man with the foreign accent."

"Thank you. I'll call him from my room."

Sophia watched as Lydia shuffled her way out of the kitchen, careful not to knock anything over with the bags of purchases she'd made on her trip. Lydia went back upstairs and sat on her bed wondering if she would, or even should call him. *Of course, I should. I spent all morning looking for him, didn't I?* But when she picked up the telephone her hand shook and she dropped it back in its recharge unit.

"What's wrong with me," she muttered and reached for the phone again. Dialing the number, she couldn't stop her hands from shaking again, but she held the phone to her ear and heard the sound of the beep each time it rang.

"Hello, hello." Frank's voice came to her crystal clear. She hesitated for a moment then identified herself.

"It's Lydia."

"I'm not available to take your call right now...."

Lydia's heart sank. After all her searching and now with Frank's phone number in her hand, she was deeply disappointed at hearing his recorded message. She waited for the beep to leave her message, but suddenly she heard him pick up on the line.

"Hello, hello."

"Frank, it's Lydia."

"Oh, hello. Are you okay?"

"Yes, thank you for asking." She paused a moment, then asked the question uppermost in her mind. "How did you know about the funeral and how to find me?"

"It was in the papers."

"Oh, yes, of course. Silly me. I forgot about that."

"Well, I saw your name and showed up to see if it was really you. I hope you don't mind."

"Oh, no. It was just a surprise to see you there."

"You didn't say you were married."

"I was trying to get my head clear. I wasn't expecting to meet anyone here in Carmel and didn't know what to say when we met."

"So when I held you last night, it wasn't just me you were rejecting, it was because you had just lost your husband."

"Yes. Please don't take it personally."

"I won't, now. I was a little put off at first. I thought I'd lost my boyish charm." She could sense that he was smiling on the other end of the phone line. "I understand now."

Lydia suppressed a laugh. Frank *was* charming. Any other time she would have reacted differently toward him. Any other time, she would have welcomed his attention.

"No, you haven't lost your charm," she said. "I just wasn't prepared...."

"Say no more. Suppose I give you a few days to yourself and then, when the time is right, we meet for lunch somewhere?"

"I—I don't know. Give me some time to think about it."

"Certainly, luv. I wouldn't want to press you, it's just that you're the nicest lady I've met since I've been here."

"Call me tomorrow." Lydia instantly regretted saying that because she sounded too eager to see him. She hadn't told him about finding his painting or hoping to find him somewhere along the strip.

"All right, I will. And...don't be concerned. I'm not wanting to rush you into anything. We'll take it easy and get to know each other before doing anything foolish."

"Foolish?"

"Yeah, foolish. Like falling for each other too quickly."

"Just friends?

"Yes…for now."

They hung up and Lydia fell back on the bed, lightheaded. Her heart pumped fast and she felt a rush of warmth run all over her body. *Was it really this easy to fall for someone you just met?* She didn't know what to think. Growing up, she'd only had one boyfriend before meeting Josh and the most they had ever done was kiss and pet each other. She was still a virgin when Josh came along and their romance had been like setting a lighted match to a can of gasoline. The explosion started with a kiss and ended up with marriage and a honeymoon in Mexico City. The honeymoon didn't stop entirely. Life with Josh had been one party after another. *What would it be like with Frank?*

Quieter, perhaps. She wasn't the wheeler dealer type like Josh and Frank didn't seem that way at all. He was a liberal arts major, he'd said. *Artists are low key and moody, aren't they?* Her mind whirled with useless thoughts. The only constant was that Frank had thought enough about her to check out the funeral and to see how she was holding up. In fact—her mind flashed back to the graveyard scene—he even helped hold her up when she slipped.

While the Angels Slept

So many thoughts were giving her a headache. Lydia got out of bed and went downstairs again to the kitchen. A nice glass of milk, perhaps, would help her slip away into an afternoon nap. As she approached the kitchen she heard Vito and Sophia talking. *What were they saying? Something about the art theft in Paris?* No, she must have heard wrong. Nevertheless, she crept back toward the stairs.

"We can meet Pietro next week," Sophia said. "Our man here is set to go?"

"Yes," Vito said. "I passed him a note this morning right after I talked to our son."

"So...hush, I thought I heard something."

Lydia didn't want the Fanuccis to know she had been eavesdropping. She knew something in their conversation sounded odd. *Leave it alone,* she told herself. *Ignorance is bliss,* her mother always said. Another saying scratched away at the back of her mind: *Curiosity killed the cat.* Lydia paused at the bottom of the stairs and listened.

The Fanuccis were still in the kitchen, still talking, but not about art any longer. Sophia was asking her husband what he wanted for supper that night. She acted like she hadn't heard Lydia come downstairs. *Better safe than sorry.* Lydia thought. She climbed the stairs as quietly as she could and slipped back into her bedroom.

Chapter 12

P IETRO FANUCCI WOKE EARLY. He looked over at the blonde woman still curled up asleep in his bed and smiled as he remembered the passion they had shared just a few hours earlier. He rolled his body carefully toward her, making sure he did not wake her. He slipped the lime-green sheet down past her shoulder and watched as tiny goose bumps formed on her skin as the coolness of the morning rushed over the bare spot of her arm where the sheet had been.

She had shown him to a good steak house. The meal pleased him, as did the English ale. He wasn't a heavy drinker but he bought several rounds. She was a spunky girl it turned out and enjoyed dancing with Pietro and two or three other chaps, all with his approval. Pietro was not a jealous man. Especially confident in the charms he had with women, he knew he would be taking the blonde to his room after she had done her night of flirting. Besides, he cared nothing for her beyond having a good time. He would fly away and leave her with a good memory, then be on his own again until the next time he needed a woman.

Vive la différence! That was Pietro's motto. He admired beautiful women but he knew that he was not the type of man to be snared by just one woman. Not with his lifestyle. He liked traveling around the world, sometimes for pleasure, often for profit, and occasionally out of necessity to avoid being arrested. He was known to many police agencies around the world, though not necessarily by name. In Canada, his name would not raise an eyebrow. It was the one country where Pietro had committed no crime. He was just another citizen there. No wanted posters on him under his name.

There was a knock at the door. Pietro rose quietly from the bed and got dressed. Edward Craven stood there with a smile on his face. He was looking over Pietro's shoulder at the blonde still asleep on the bed. Pietro had pulled the sheet completely off her and Craven could see her naked body turned away from him. The graceful curve of her hip rose upwards from a well-tapered set of legs she had curled child-like beneath her. She had wrapped her arms around herself in reaction to the coldness she felt. The temperature that morning was six degrees Celsius, a little above forty degrees Fahrenheit. The temperature in the room had been warmer, of course, but now with the door open the woman responded to the additional chill encircling her body.

Pietro gathered his travel bag and the six rolls of canvasses and handed them to Craven who took them to the small Ford Anglia. Pietro turned back to the woman, stepped closer to the bed and leaned down to whisper in her eat.

"Thank you for a lovely evening," he said.

The blonde looked up at him with dreamy

Marilyn Monroe eyes and smiled those luscious lips of hers at him. He had bruised them all night long with his voracious kisses and tasted the sweetness of her tongue with his own.

She had been a wonderful lover and as he drew back from her, he watched her close her eyes again and return her head to her pillow. Pietro slipped a hundred euros from his wallet and left the money on the table beside her. Before leaving the room, Pietro pulled the sheet back over her body and kissed her on the cheek. He closed the door quietly behind him as he stepped outside.

Pietro looked at the sky. Fate had almost been against him this trip. A thin coating of fine light ash covered the ground, left there by the eruption of the Eyjafjallajokull volcano in Iceland, which closed parts of UK air space in the first week of May and again during the middle of the month, causing some flight delays and cancellations.

But luck was with him and Lydd Airport had resumed normal operation after a light rainfall on the seventeenth of the month.

"You're all set, then?" Craven asked as Pietro climbed inside the car.

"As much as I'll ever be. I just want to get home."

"How was the lady?" Craven cast him an evil smile.

"They all look alike after awhile," Pietro replied. "But this one was a charmer."

"She looked pretty good from what I could see."

"She was all that and more."

Airline security scanned Pietro's parcels and visually inspected his tote bag, but passed him through without question other than asking him if he had any weapons on him. He jokingly produced a safety razor and was surprised when the security officer took the blade from it along with his pack of unused Wilkinson Sword double-edged razor blades and discarded them into a large container.

"Next time, use a disposable," the man told him. "We let those pass."

The flight to Vancouver, Canada took a little more than nine hours. Pietro had left a car at the airport and tossed his packages in the front seat. He laughed at the thought that he had just flown with over a hundred million dollars worth of stolen art and not a single person had bothered to check it.

He arrived home a little tired from the trip but none the worse for wear. He was almost thirty-eight and not getting any younger but still kept himself in good shape. Nevertheless, his first action upon entering his home was to head for the bathroom. His bladder had been giving him trouble all year and he desperately had to empty it before he called his parents.

"Dad," he said as Vito Fanucci picked up the telephone. "I'm home. I picked up some swell things on my trip to Europe that I can't wait to show you."

"We'll be up there next week, son. You had no trouble making your connections?"

"Not a bit. I stayed overnight at a nice hotel and caught an early flight. The trip was long and tiring, but I'm here now and I promise to be all rested up by the time you and momma get here next week. And, this time I'm going to beat you at chess."

"That will never happen," Vito said laughing at him. "See you soon."

"Goodbye, poppa."

Chapter 13

SOPHIA STOOD OVER LYDIA'S BED watching her sleep. Lydia slowly opened her eyes, stretched and smiled up at the woman. She'd slept all that evening and through the night. A quick "Good morning" was answered with a nod of the head and the placement of the breakfast tray on Lydia's lap.

"I told you this was going to spoil me."

"I want to spoil you. You need to put a few pounds on those bones." Sophia spoke softly but without her usual vibrant, cheerful emotion. She opened the curtain to let light into the room, then placed the newspaper by Lydia's side and sat down on the bed to talk.

"How long do you plan to stay with us?"

"I don't know, for sure. Is there a problem?"

"Vito and I were planning a vacation for next week. We have a son, Peter, in Canada. We usually see him this time of year."

"Do I need to leave, then."

"Well, we could arrange for someone to be here to look after you."

"My goodness! I'm not deathly ill. If that's all you're worried about, I can certainly take care of myself for a week."

Sophia laughed. "I didn't mean you couldn't. But you're our guest, at least a guest of our employer, we have an obligation to you."

"I'll be fine. Take your vacation and just tell me what to do in case something needs done around here. I know how to use the phone to call a repairman."

"Don't hold it against us; we were thinking of your needs."

"That's a relief. I thought you were kicking me out of here and into the street."

Both of them laughed. Sophia seemed her old jolly self again. "No, no, no. Nothing like that," the older woman assured her. Lydia finished her breakfast and Sophia removed the tray.

Lydia wondered what she would do with herself today? Shopping seemed to be in order even though she'd done that yesterday. *You know the rules,* she thought, *EVERY DAY IS SHOPPING DAY.*

Actually, it didn't matter. All she needed was an excuse, anything to get out of the house on such a beautiful day. She got up, got dressed and went downstairs to say goodbye to Sophia then she practically ran out the door, eager to lose herself in the bright sunshine that, hot as it was, seemed to melt her troubles away.

Roaming around Carmel later that day, Lydia found a neat little boutique between Ocean and Seventh Avenue selling art, pottery and some ornate types of glassware and a charming old book store between Fifth and Sixth Avenues. She spent hours there, at both stores, and came away from the book store with a copy of Beatrix

Potter's original twenty-three Peter Rabbit tales and verses for just thirty dollars. The deluxe edition had all of Potter's original illustrations, both color and black and white. Lydia had loved these stories as a little girl and remembered the little books she owned, a collection which her mother had thrown away when Lydia was in high school.

Lydia took the scenic route at Carmel Bay and worked her way back up past Carmel Mission and turned south on Highway One in the direction of Big Sur. At noon, she parked at the same restaurant where she'd met Marge and Mitch two days before.

Marge wasn't there, but Mitch had taken up a table near a rock wall and had surrounded himself with a throng of perky teenage girls all rocking back and forth to his rendition of the Peter, Paul and Mary tune, *Puff the Magic Dragon.*

"He's a pretty good singer, isn't he?" A starry-eyed waitress took Lydia's order.

A moment later the waitress returned with a plate of fish and chips and a glass of white wine. The woman paced the plate of food in front of Lydia without taking her eyes off the young man.

Lydia agreed to herself that Mitch was as talented as he was good looking. She would have liked him more except for his crude personality. Still, when he'd finished the song and noticed her, she smiled as he approached and plopped himself down in a chair next to her.

He was wearing the same cargo pants and

blue denim shirt she'd seen him wearing the first time they met. He draped a leg over the arm of the chair he took and Lydia noticed the fine, blond hairs on his legs; almost as fine as a woman's who hadn't shaved her legs. The hairs stood out against the deep tan of his skin. His calves bulged beneath the frayed edges of his pants and she looked up at his arms, which also were firm as if he worked out often, but she noticed his chest and shoulders were a little less developed than she had expected. Still, he was downright handsome in his body and in his face, and she liked his carefree way of holding himself in a slouch in the chair.

"Well, did you come back for more of me?"

"You're rather full of yourself, aren't you? Where's Marge?"

"Don't know. We only see each other occasionally. We're not lovers, you know."

"Sorry. I rather thought that you were."

"Really? Because we're so familiar with each other? Well, we have tossed the bed sheets around a time or two, but we're not serious about each other."

"Oh, I see."

"Oh, you do? Then you approve of two people taking a romp or two in bed? Without commitment, I mean?"

"That's up to the two people, I suppose. If they like each other and aren't serious…."

"I could get serious with you, you know."

Lydia blushed. "Don't say that." She took another sip of wine to steady her nerves.

"Why not?"

"I wasn't trying to lead you on."

"Too bad. I wish you were."

She blushed again and held her glass on the table between them as a symbolic barrier, as if that would keep Mitch away from her.

He leaned across the table and leered at her, flashing a row of stunningly white teeth. "Don't you find me the least bit attractive?"

She laughed and shook her head 'no' but had to lower her eyes to hide the lie that the gesture implied.

His face screwed up in a look of confusion. He looked like a little boy who didn't understand why he shouldn't play with himself.

"Oh, I suppose so," she finally said. *Damn right I do, but I'm not about to let you know that.* "But I wouldn't want you to get the wrong idea."

"Oh, I see. You're not *that* kind of a girl." His face relaxed, looking more friendly and self-assured.

"It's not that," she said, her voice sounding more defensive that she had intended. "I'm just not looking for any kind of a relationship right now."

"How about a five-minute quickie, then?"

"Oh, hush! You're terrible."

"Yeah, I am. But I made you laugh."

He had done that. Lydia's smile stretched across her face. She found Mitch more charming the more time she spent with him. She wasn't as bold as Marge in how she conversed with him.

She envied Marge in her unabashed openness; yet, something told Lydia not to go too deep in unknown waters.

"I have to go soon as I finish my dinner."

"That's all right. So do I." He arose, grabbed his guitar and grabbed her hand, shaking it lightly. "Glad we ran into each other again. Sorry if I was too rough for you, that's just my way." He left and Lydia quickly swallowed another large sip of wine.

He really is full of himself, she thought, *but in a nice sort of way.*

After dropping his guitar in his bright blue Mustang, Mitch looked back toward the door of the restaurant. He had a plan and he had to hurry. He walked around Lydia's Mini Cooper and dropped to the ground near the driver's side rear tire. He fumbled with the stem cap until it came off, then with a push on the valve release with a ballpoint pen, the air oozed out of the tire until it was mostly flat. He quickly replaced the cap and walked away, waiting by his car until Lydia came outside.

She paid for her meal and headed toward the parking lot. Her shoulders sagged when she saw the flattened tire on the Mini Cooper. She kicked the gravel in the parking lot and looked all about for help.

"Got a spare?" Mitch stood behind her looking down at the tire.

"No, I—I took it out before leaving Los Angeles so I could pack more stuff inside it."

"Ah, not good planning. Listen, I know these folks, you can leave the car here and they'll keep an eye on it for you. I can drop you where you want to go. You can call for a tow and have a service station repair the tire. Better yet, I'll go inside and call for you. There's a place just down the road that's got a wrecker. I know the guy who works there, good guy, won't charge you an arm and a leg 'cause it's me doing the calling. I'll leave you a number and you can call me when it's done; I'll pick you up and take you there to pick up your car. And I won't charge you for the taxi service." He smiled broadly, his teeth shining in the bright sunlight; his hair fluttered in the breeze, long strands of it floated in front of his face, covering one eye.

Lydia looked at the flat tire and nodded her head. She could have called for roadside service but she didn't want to wait around and, besides, she wanted to get her packages home.

"All right. I'll give you directions." She retrieved her packages from the Mini Cooper and made sure it was locked up tight.

"I'll just be a minute," Mitch said, handing her the keys and pointing to a bright blue Mustang parked behind her. "I'll tell them to send a service truck." He disappeared inside the restaurant for a moment. When he returned, Lydia had already seated herself in the Mustang and stared woefully at her poor flat-tired car.

"Okay," Mitch said as he settled into the driver's seat. "I called for a repair truck and they said they'd take care of it for you. You can pick it up tomorrow. Is that okay?"

Lydia gave a nod of her head. She was grateful she was with someone who knew the area and knew who to call.

"Now, where to, lady?"

They drove along the coastline with Mitch talking almost non-stop. Lydia barely said a word, barely had an opening in his speech even if she wanted to speak. She didn't, not until they got near her house and she said, "Turn here." They pulled into the driveway of the villa and Lydia stepped out.

"Do you want to come in for a drink or something?" She felt obligated to pay him back in some way.

"That would be nice," he replied unbuckling his seat belt.

They stepped inside and Lydia called for Sophia. No answer. She called for Vito, but again there was no answer.

"I guess they're out."

"You have servants?"

"Caretakers. They don't work for me. This is a friend's house. He and his wife are letting me stay here a few days. I'm sort of on vacation."

"That sounds nice and convenient. Hey, how about that drink?"

"Sure thing. Follow me."

She led the way to the den and found the liquor cabinet. She asked him what he wanted to drink.

Mitch glanced around at the furniture in the room. It was a dark mahogany and leather combination and he nodded his head in approval at the styling of it. The walls were lined with books and he strolled past them looking at their titles but otherwise seeming uninterested in them.

Heavy curtains made the room darker, but the lighting was adequate to see by. A natural rock fireplace covered one wall and a bumper pool table took up the center of the den. Mitch stood by the table rolling a ball against one of the side banks, trying to sink it in the hole opposite where he stood.

"What will you have?" Lydia asked.

"Oh, some bourbon, I guess. I'm not really that much of a drinker. I'd just like to sit and talk with you for awhile."

Lydia splashed a jigger of bourbon in a glass and handed it to Mitch. She poured herself a glass of white wine. She followed Mitch as he casually plopped himself down on the dark leather sofa and patted the seat beside him. She still felt tense as she approached him and sat down, and thought the wine might help her relax. It did, but not until she had finished it.

Mitch downed the rest of his glass and got up to grab the bottle himself, refilling it with a double-shot this time. He held up the wine bottle and Lydia nodded her head. He came back to the sofa and splashed some of the clear liquid in her glass. He sat the bottle down on the table in front of her.

"I usually don't drink much either," she said. "Only when I'm at a party."

"Got any music? We'll make it a party."

Before she could say anything, Mitch spotted the stereo controls, jumped up and walked over to them. He twisted the dial and found a radio station playing a slow dance tune. He approached her, took her in his arms to pull her from the sofa and said, "Let's dance. You do know how to dance, don't you?"

She felt a tingle rush through her body and wondered if it was from the wine she'd consumed or from Mitch's arms around her. He shuffled his feet and she followed. He pulled her closer. Lydia felt a little uncomfortable, but remembered that Josh had always approved of her dancing close with other men. Mitch was no target for investment, but dancing close to him seemed as natural as all the other times she'd played the game for her husband.

"You dance very well," Mitch said, brushing his lips past her ear. "You must've had plenty of practice, pretty girl like you. I'll bet you got asked to dance a lot at all those parties you must have gone to in school."

"Thank you," Lydia felt a little odd hearing Mitch talk about her like he was, but it was true, she liked to dance and Josh had not minded, even encouraged her to dance. "Thank you," she repeated. "You dance very well, yourself." Mitch pulled her tightly into him. Lydia felt another tingle creep up her spine. Mitch was holding her so tightly that she felt a movement between them, a stiffness between his legs that she instantly recognized. She tried to pull back but he wouldn't let her go.

"C'mon, baby. Don't pull away. I know you like me."

"Mitch, please let me go."

"It's a party, remember? We're going to have some fun."

He trapped her against the back of the sofa and held her there, leaning into her. His hands roamed to her breasts and squeezed them. Forcing his hips forward, he rubbed himself between her legs and covered her mouth with his, piercing her lips with his tongue and seeking out her own.

A danger flag sent a quiver through Lydia's body. She broke the kiss and shouted at him. "Mitch, please!"

He bent her over the back of the sofa, so far that her head touched the lower seat cushion. He forced himself between her legs keeping them apart and ran his hand under the short skirt she wore.

"Mitch, no! I mean, NO!"

He grabbed her by the throat and snarled at her as he pushed back her skirt and tore away her underpants. When he had done so, he reached behind his back and pulled a brightly polished knife from under his waist band. He held it under her throat and hissed a warning at her.

"Look here, you little prick teaser. I didn't come here for just a drink and a goodbye kiss. I'm gonna give you the best time you ever had. You can give me what I want or I'll take it the hard way. You understand that?"

Frightened now, she nodded. Mitch held her down with one hand, placed the knife away from them on the back of the sofa and snatched open his belt. He unzipped his cargo pants in a hurry and pulled them down. He wore no underwear and his manhood sprang forth at full attention.

"Please, don't."

He didn't seem to listen. His face glowed red and he twisted his lips in utter frustration as he tried to enter her and couldn't. Lydia's body had slid further into the sofa and the back of the sofa prevented him from following. He lunged at her with great force and for a brief moment felt himself nearly penetrate her precious opening.

The force of his pressure didn't achieve what he wanted, however, but the vibration he caused knocked the knife off the back of the sofa. The blade landed on the seat near Lydia's hand. She instinctively wrapped her fingers around its handle and pressed the point against Mitch's stomach. She shoved hard and heard a soft ripping sounded as the blade entered his body.

Mitch's eyes crossed as he looked down at the blood pouring from his belly. He looked at her and Lydia was afraid he would take the knife away from her and kill her. She shoved again. This time the ripping sound was louder because he had pulled back a little way from her. Still holding the knife between their closely pressed bodies, she slashed away and heard him groan in agony. Mitch stepped back and looked at the front of his pale blue shirt.

Lydia saw streams of blood flowing down his chest, down to one of his bare legs. She screamed. Mitch fell to the floor without making a sound. He pulled his legs up under him in a fetal position and stopped moving. Soon he stopped breathing.

Del Garrett

Chapter 14

LYDIA LOOKED AT MITCH lying there on the floor. His blood seeped slowly from the knife wounds in his body. She dropped the bloody blade on the sofa and stepped away from his body. Her hands rose to her mouth and tears poured from her eyes. She asked herself, *What am I going to do now?* She reached for the telephone to call the police, but her trembling hand stopped before picking up the receiver. *They will arrest me for murder,* she thought. She dug in her purse and found the crumpled up piece of paper with Frank's number on it. Hastily, she dialed the number and got a busy signal. She redialed and this time heard the sound of his phone ringing as her call went through. Frank picked up on the third ring.

"Hello, hello."

"Frank, it's Lydia."

"What's the matter? You sound like you've been crying."

"Frank...I'm in trouble."

"Where are you?"

"At the villa. Frank, I've—"

"Don't say anything. I'll be right there."

Lydia heard a click as the line went dead, then silence. She didn't know how far away Frank was or how long it would take him to get there. The clock ticked off the minutes, each one seemed like hours to her; the ticking of the clock echoed throughout the room. She sat beside the hearth in front of the fireplace and looked at Mitch's body, thinking all that had happened was unreal, as if she expected him to sit up, say it was all a joke and laugh at her. He didn't do that, of course, but several times she could have sworn that he did. Her mind imagined all sorts of possibilities. She had a vision of two burly policemen knocking down the front door and dragging her off, kicking and screaming, while Mitch's body rose up from the floor and followed her zombie-like outside to the patrol car like some old black and white B-movie. She expected at any moment she might take the knife to her own throat and take her own life.

Finally, after what seemed like an eternity, Lydia heard tires squeal to a halt in the driveway and a frantic knocking on the door. She hurried to the door and opened it. Frank stepped in, took her in his arms and comforted her while asking what happened.

"I—I've killed someone."

"What?" Surely he hadn't heard her correctly, but she repeated herself and fell into his arms again.

"Where?"

Lydia stepped away from Frank and pointed toward the den. He followed her and when she stopped by the door, refusing to enter any farther, he stepped around her and looked inside. At first Frank didn't see Mitch's body behind the sofa. He stepped deeper into the room and saw Mitch's heels, then legs, and finally his whole body and the pool of blood that had gathered beneath him. Calmly, Frank knelt down and placed a finger alongside Mitch's carotid artery to check for a pulse. Finding none, he looked up at Lydia and shook his head.

"*Crikey*, girl. What have you done?"

"He…he tried to rape me. He pulled a knife on me and…."

Frank stood up and looked down at the body. "Did you call the police?"

"No, I started to but I was afraid they would arrest me."

Frank didn't answer right away. Lydia could tell he was thinking about all the possibilities. She waited. Never being involved in anything like this, Lydia wanted Frank to tell her what to do.

"That's just exactly what the cops would do," he said, "arrest you, I mean. He's a local. I know him. I'm afraid you've got big trouble, girl. His father is a big shot here; owns half the damn tourist traps in the city."

"What am I going to do?" She was shaking all over, tears flooding her eyes, waiting to fall. She'd balled up her hands and pressed them to her cheeks.

"Only thing to do. We dump the body somewhere. Where's the old couple?"

"I—I don't know."

"We've got to move fast, then, before they come back. Where's the bathroom? I need the shower curtain to wrap the body in.'"

Lydia pointed the way down the hall. Frank found the bathroom and carefully removed the shower curtain from the clips holding it to the curtain rod. He ran back into the den and shoved the plastic sheet beneath one side of Mitch's body. He hastily pulled up Mitch's pants and rolled the body over onto the plastic, and rolled him once again to complete the wrap.

"Get this blood cleaned up while I'm gone," he ordered Lydia as he lifted Mitch's body, hoisting it onto his shoulder and lugging it out to the Mustang. Seeing that her car wasn't in the driveway, he figured rightly that the muscle car belonged to the man she had killed. He placed the body on the hood of the car and unwrapped the plastic enough so that he could fumble through Mitch's pockets until he found the car keys. A click of a button on the electronic key and the lock popped open on the driver's door.

Frank popped the trunk and tossed Mitch's body inside. There was little room in there. He bent Mitch's legs back and wedged the head forward. The body slumped at an odd angle but it fit well enough for Frank to slam down the lid.

"What do I do about this?" Lydia had followed him outside carrying Mitch's knife. In her state of shock she was pointing the weapon straight at Frank. He grabbed the blade, pushing it to one side, and carefully pulled it from her fingers.

"Did you wipe your prints off?"

"No, I didn't think about that."

"I'll do it when I get rid of the body."

Frank stuck the knife down inside Mitch's waist band and pulled his shirt over it. Jumping into the Mustang, he peeled out of the driveway without looking back. He headed for Big Sur, that long stretch of road with lots of open space to it, plenty of places to dump the car and body. Even with traffic, Frank figured he could get far enough away from the house to make the cops think when they found the body that it was just a random crime. He figured to drop off the car and body without arousing too much suspicion, and catch a ride back after the deed was done.

His mind raced as he headed out along the Pacific Coast Highway. He would park the car, place the body inside under the steering wheel and place the knife on the floorboard after wiping his and Lydia's prints away. The police would think the killer dropped the blade accidentally or just to get rid of it. If there weren't any witnesses to see Frank set the body behind the steering wheel, the crime would probably go unsolved.

The blood on the shower curtain could be washed off in the ocean. It was getting dark so Frank felt more at ease with himself as he drove. He hadn't noticed his speed, however. Mustangs are built for speed. Quickly, he looked at the speedometer and saw he was ten miles over the limit. He forced himself to slow down, to catch his breath and to act as normal as he could. *Just out for an evening's ride, officer. What's that,*

that thumping noise? Oh, nothing, just a dead guy in the trunk. Crikey, how did he get himself into these kind of fixes? Slowing down the car turned out to be a good thing because less than a minute after he dropped to the legal speed limit a California Highway Patrol car passed him heading toward Carmel.

The sky was dark now as Frank turned off the road and parked the car on the beach. He slipped off his shoes, tying the laces together and slung them around his neck. He did this so he wouldn't leave any tracks in the sand. In his socks, he stepped to the rear of the Mustang, opened the trunk and turned his back toward the highway as a car speeded by. After the car passed, he hefted Mitch's body from the trunk, propped him up against the car and stripped the shower curtain off the body. Quickly shoving the body behind the wheel, Frank pulled the knife from Mitch's waistband and used his T-shirt to wipe it down before tossing it inside the car. Then, as an afterthought, Frank pulled Mitch's billfold out his pocket and grabbed what cash was in it, leaving the credit cards and other items untouched. Using his T-shirt again, Frank wiped his prints from the wallet and let it drop in Mitch's lap. *This will make it look like a robbery*, he thought. He shut the door, grabbed up the shower curtain and went back to the trunk to shut it. Another car passed at a slow pace and Frank, once again, turned his face away so the driver couldn't see him. He then ran to the edge of the water, dropped the shower curtain in and swished it around, hoping all the blood would wash away. Folding the curtain as tightly as he could, Frank ran down the surf, distancing himself from the scene, and ran up again to a spot farther down the road where he paused long enough to brush the sand off his now wet socks and put his shoes back on, then stuffed the shower curtain under his arm and headed for a grocery store he had passed a mile back. At the store, he hid the curtain behind a bush, went inside and purchased some beer and chips. When he retrieved the curtain, he emptied the sack and stuffed it down inside the grocery bag. He placed the beer and chips on top of the curtain and headed back toward the villa.

Lydia scrubbed the hardwood floor with soap and water, but the blood stain was still there. She found some bleach and used that. The bleach cut the stain until she could barely see it. Vito and Sophia were still gone, thankfully, but she worked as hard and as fast as she could, worrying they might return at any moment. She hoped to be finished by the time they returned. When she satisfied herself that she had got all the blood up, Lydia went to the bathroom and rinsed out the towels she'd used. Next, she carried them to the washing machine, dropped them in and added laundry detergent. She turned the machine on and walked back into the den.

Just as she did that, Frank rang the doorbell and she let him in. They sat for a long time not talking. Frank opened one of the beers in the sack and offered one to Lydia. She shook her head. He looked at the hardwood floor where the blood had been and nodded his head in approval at the cleanup job she had done. Anyone looking at the spot on the floor wouldn't be able to tell anything was wrong. He looked at the rest of the room and saw the glasses Lydia and Mitch had used. Frank carried them to the wet bar and washed them, replacing them in their spot in the cabinet. He removed the shower curtain from the paper sack and hung it up in the bathroom.

"Everything's taken care of," he said. "I'm going to leave now, but I'll call you tomorrow."

"What am I going to do?" Her voice shook, she started crying again.

"Nothing. Nothing happened." He grabbed her by the shoulders and shook her gently. "All you have to do is go to bed. If the police drop by and ask you about your car, tell them what you told me, that it had a flat and you had it towed in. Tomorrow, I'll come by and pick you up and we'll go get your car. Everything looks normal. Don't worry. Go to bed."

He kissed her and left. Lydia looked around and turned off the lights, then went to her bedroom and got dressed in her nightgown. She couldn't fall asleep until early morning. She never heard Vito and Sophia arrive home.

Chapter 15

ON THE FOLLOWING MORNING, Sophia woke Lydia wanting to know if she was all right. She did not bring a breakfast tray this time. Her warm, dark eyes were clouded with worry and she reached out a hand to touch the girl's cheek as if she were sick. In her other hand were the towels from the wash, still wet, and each bearing a faint stain of blood.

"I found these in the washing machine. Are you all right?"

Thinking rapidly, Lydia told her she'd had a nose bleed in the den the night before and used the towels to clean the floor.

"Do you often have nose bleeds?"

"No, not often. I don't know what caused this one." Lydia avoided looking at Sophia. The housekeeper noticed that but said nothing for a moment. The silence seemed longer than a moment to Lydia.

Finally Sophia asked, "Is there anything you wish to tell me?"

"No. No, I'm fine." *Does she know? How could she know?*

"Very well. I'll fix your breakfast now. You do feel like eating?"

"Oh, yes, of course." Lydia was glad the questions seemed to be over. She felt relieved as Sophia left the room. Lydia hated having to lie to her.

While the Angels Slept

Moments later, Sophia returned with a tray and placed it across Lydia's lap. Thinking back on what had happened, Lydia found she had no appetite, but she forced herself to eat some of the eggs and toast to prove to Sophia that she was feeling normal. She ate all of the bacon because it smelled so good and tasted even better than it smelled. By the time she had finished the bacon and half the toast, Lydia was feeling her old self again. The guilt had gone. She knew she had only been protecting herself and the little white lies she told to Sophia were just to keep the woman from worrying..

Frank arrived shortly after that without calling. Sophia questioned him but Frank feigned ignorance of anything wrong. Sophia had practically accused him of attacking Lydia. Frank honestly denied anything like that.

"I never touched her," he said. "It's not my style to force myself on a woman. She's told me all about her husband's accident. If I tried anything with her it would cause a problem I don't want. I have other plans for her besides having her in bed."

"That's another thing," Sophia said with a sternness that caused Frank to stiffen, "I want you to forget about fleecing her. Mr. Atherton pays you plenty for your talent. You don't need to steal from this girl."

"You don't understand," he replied. "It's in my nature. I grew up with nothing but the smell of fish on my hands. I can't live like my old man. I do what I have to do. Besides, rich as she is, she'll never miss it."

Sophia gave him a final warning look and turned away. Frank waited in the living room while she went up the stairs to announce his presence. Lydia was almost dressed when Sophia knocked on the door.

"That young man who stayed here the other night is downstairs." Sophia tried to look as cheerful as possible. "He said he came to pick you up to carry you to get your car. Did you have an accident?"

"No, just a flat tire. I didn't want to wait around while some mechanic fixed it. Frank was nice enough to say he'd come by and pick me up this morning."

Sophia wondered if that were true, but seeing Lydia was not apprehensive in any way decided that her instincts must be wrong. She cared about Lydia and didn't want to see anyone hurt her. "Well, he's waiting for you downstairs and he seems nervous as a cat about something. You'd better watch his driving so you don't end up in an accident."

Lydia assured Sophia that everything would be all right. She finished dressing and looked at her reflection in the mirror. She had chosen a full-skirted black dress with a hem that ended just above her knees. The top sported a short collar trimmed in a small white rope along the edge that ran down the front and off the side ending at the waist. The skirt below was totally black and had no such trim. Lydia fastened a white belt around her waist and hurried down to meet Frank. They said their goodbyes to Sophia and left.

"Did you say anything to her?" Lydia looked worried.

"No, of course not. Did you?"

"She found a blood stain on the towels I'd placed in the washer. It didn't all come out. I told her I'd had a nose bleed and used the towels to wipe up a spot on the floor."

"That was quick thinking. By the way, where are we going? I mean, where's your car?"

"Oh, my God. I don't even know. Mitch made the call to the service station."

"Well, we'll go by the restaurant where you left it and see what they can tell us."

Lydia tried to remember everything that Mitch had said. She brightened up and told Frank, "He said there was a service station 'just up the road' from the café. Maybe we'll be lucky and spot it on the way."

"Okay, we'll look for it. I know a garage on the strip near the restaurant. They have a wrecker there. Maybe we'll find your car there."

Frank drove the speed limit. Lydia noticed that whatever had caused Sophia to be worried about his nerves didn't seem to affect the way he drove. He slowed the car along a stretch of the highway not far from the villa. Two police cars and a county medical examiner's SUV were parked off the road next to Mitch's dark blue Mustang. The medical examiner and an attendant were busy loading Mitch's body inside the back of their vehicle while the two policemen were examining the Mustang. The trunk was open as well as both doors. A Crime Scene Unit approached from the north and pulled off the road. Two technicians got out of their SUV and approached the detectives. A gentle breeze swept lazily across the ocean's surface causing the canvass wrap over Mitch's body to flap back and forth in the wind.

"Is that—?"

"Yes, I know this spot is close to the house but I didn't want to drive too far with a dead body in the trunk."

"What shall we do?"

"Nothing. We find your car and drive it home."

Which is what they did. Frank drove straight to the garage he knew where they found Lydia's car sitting outside in plain sight. They parked and went inside. Frank asked about the car and a guy named Joe—his name was embroidered on his shirt—checked a clipboard full of papers.

"Yep, tow job and a flat tire. Tow job's sixty-five and the flat came to twenty, with tax."

Lydia paid the man with a credit card. She fished the keys out of her purse and unlocked the door of the Mini Cooper.

"You okay to drive?" Frank leaned inside the car and helped her adjust her seat belt.

"Yes, but I don't want to go straight home. Sophia seemed to suspect something about the blood. I don't want to answer any more of her questions just yet."

"Do you think she really suspects anything?"

Lydia thought for a moment. "No, I don't think so…but, then, I don't really know for sure."

"Well, stick to your story about the nose bleed if she says anything."

"Let's go someplace quiet."

"The restaurant just up the road?"

"No, not there. I'd feel too creeped out, like maybe Mitch's ghost was hanging out there watching us. Let's find another place."

Frank laughed at the thought of Mitch and his ghostly guitar serenading people.

"Okay, we'll go up to the mall area," he said. "Lots of people up there, we can get lost in the crowd."

"All right. Sounds nice. I'll follow you." She drove steadily all the way to the mall. Her guilty conscience still bothered her a little, but the whole incident had a settling effect as well, making her numb as she had felt during Josh's funeral.

"You didn't do anything wrong," Frank told her as they sat in Starbucks drinking frappuccinos with whipped cream. Lydia had the mocha base; Frank had the girl behind the counter give his an extra shot of espresso.

She thought about what Frank had said. "I know," she told him. "It's just what we did afterward."

"*We* didn't. I did. There's no connection to you unless someone saw the Mustang at your house, or saw the two of you at the restaurant."

"Nobody that I know saw us together. The Fanuccis weren't there. Nobody can see the villa's driveway from the road. And nobody came to the door."

"So it sounds like there are no witnesses."

"Sounds like."

"Then we should be in the clear. Besides, it was self-defense. Even if the police somehow put the whole thing together, you could always tell them the truth. It would hold up under a lie detector."

"I wish I would have gone ahead and called them. I feel so guilty this way."

"Put it aside. He got what he deserved."

Try as she might, Lydia found it hard not to think about Mitch. Frank changed the subject several times but Lydia kept returning to what had happened. Finally in exasperation he told her, "Go home, get some rest. Answer some letters, or write some if you don't have any to respond to. Do *something* to take your mind off what's happened."

"That's all I can do, isn't it?"

"Everything will pass."

"I hope you're right." She wasn't sure, though. Frank was just another person like her, not a lawyer like Peter Manning, and not necessarily a man of the world like Raymond Atherton. She put so much trust in a man who was nothing more than an artist and a part-time restaurant worker?

"I'm sure I'm right," he said, "but I have a suggestion. Just in case anything goes wrong, I think you'd best pick a good lawyer. Don't make contact unless you have to, but just be prepared in case you need to. And things could get nasty with your bank account. In case the cops freeze your assets, I think you ought to prepare a war chest—draw out enough money from the bank so you'll have cash on hand as a retainer for your lawyer plus some additional expenses. I'd say ten thousand or so."

"The police would do that? Tie up my bank account?"

"You never know. Rather safe than sorry, they say."

Lydia left the mall and drove back along the Pacific Coast Highway. When she got to the spot in the road where Frank had dumped the car and the body, she slowed down to watch a tow truck hook up the Mustang and to see the police milling about. A plain clothes type looked in Lydia's direction so she sped up, continuing her journey.

When she arrived back at the villa, Sophia already had lunch prepared, *flutas de polla* with roasted chicken, avocado and sour cream in a crispy corn tortilla, plus a tossed salad with lettuce, tomatoes, radishes and roasted chilies. They ate quietly. Lydia spent the afternoon in her room trying to write letters as Frank had suggested. *To whom did she have to write? Her mother? But she didn't have anything to say to her. To her lawyer, not yet.* No, writing was out of the question. She couldn't concentrate and finally gave up. She stepped outside and walked around the grounds looking at the rainbow pattern of flowers all around her.

Vito appeared to be as skilled at gardening as Sophia was in keeping house and cooking. The villa could have been a photo spread right out of Better Homes and Garden magazine. Between the house and the garage, a number of concrete stepping stones, each with the raised face of Caesar, like some gigantic Roman coin, lie embedded in a gravel pathway. On the side of the house, nestled within a bed of redwood shavings, grew bunches of red snapdragons interlaced with pungent-smelling Mexican marigolds, the kind that have a pinkish tinge to the yellow petal. The flowers stood out against a lush bed of green ground cover. By the garage, stands of alternating blue and white irises with their long, sword-like leaves bordered the base boards of the structure.

She found Vito in the back yard replacing a broken piece of flagstone in the sculpted patio. The patio's overall design was made to look like a Persian rug, with its inner placement of red bricks encircled with dark gray mortar that ran lengthwise away from the double patio doors of the house and were bounded on each end with an arch to give the whole design a gracefulness and beauty. Light gray flagstone plates had been set all around the construction, ending with a rectangle of gray mortar and a concrete encirclement which led from a common patio slab at the outside doors of the house all around to the far end, past the archway and touching a rise of slab steps, two steps deep. The top step widened into a walk-around that ended with a short, curved concrete wall, suitable for sitting upon. At the center of the steps, a box had been built extending half-way into the walk-around and half-way out over the steps. Inside this box, filled with cedar chips and gray moss, stood a concrete angel watching over the patio and, presumably, the homeowners and any guests who ventured into the patio area for the peaceful inspiration one might find in such a tranquil setting.

"Hello, Vito."

Her voice must have startled him. He dropped two broken pieces of slab and looked up suddenly with those narrow eyes of his. He curled his lower lip as if stifling something he might have said in haste.

"Oh, hello, Mrs. Taylor. Can I do something for you?" His lips formed a smile.

She remembered hearing the Fanuccis talking about artwork. Vito's garden showed he was extremely artistic in his own way. Lydia didn't know if he painted or sculpted, but he certainly had an eye for design. She wanted to ask him about what she'd heard, but she wasn't sure if she should. Besides, you don't let a shady character know you've been listening in on their private conversations. At this point, she considered the Fanuccis somehow involved in the art theft in Paris. Call it intuition. She didn't have any real proof. She reminded herself that she had enough problems of her own without playing detective.

"No. I was just admiring what you've done with the landscaping."

Vito's smile grew wider. His thick glasses magnified his narrow-slitted eyes. The oversized lens and his bald head with gray tufts of hair sticking straight out behind his ears gave his face a clown-like look about him, she thought, but in a nice way. He picked up a piece of flagstone and placed it inside the raised area of the rug-like structure.

"Good as new," she said.

"Yes. Thank you. I enjoy working on designs such as this. It's nice to have somebody notice and appreciate the effort."

"We haven't talked much, have we?"

"Oh, no. But I know 'bout all your troubles, missy. I thought it best for you and the missus to be the conversationalists here. I didn't want to seem nosy. You're s'posed to be here for a rest."

"I'm doing well, thank you. You and Sophia have made my stay a wonderful time."

"Well, if I can do anything for you, don't hesitate to ask."

"I will if I need anything. Seeing all this beauty is a big help in easing my mind."

Vito smiled at her again as Lydia walked away. He picked up the tools he'd been using and the broken stone, which he tossed in a pile behind the garage, never knowing when he might need a small piece like these.

Lydia felt better. The evening air was fresh, the scent of the flowers offered a perfume that pleased her senses, and her conversation with Vito made her feel closer to both him and Sophia. She pushed away any thoughts about stolen art or the Fanucci's involvement out of her mind. After what she'd been through with Mitch, a few stolen high-dollar paintings seemed trivial to her. She had problems of her own to consider.

What am I going to do about the house in Los Angeles? She mulled the question over in her mind but no answer came to her. She thought about Frank's suggestion of withdrawing a large amount of cash from her bank account in case the police froze her assets. She knew that international and white collar criminals were treated that way, but she had never heard of an ordinary citizen needing a war chest. It didn't seem to matter, though, because all she might lose out on would be the interest on that amount of money. Thanks to Josh, that certainly didn't seem to be a problem. Peter Manning had assured her she had enough money to do just about anything she wanted to do.

Lydia found Sophia in the kitchen and told her that she would be going back to Los Angeles in the morning to take care of some business. She packed a bag and dialed Frank's number. He wasn't doing anything important and asked if he could go with her just so they could spend some time together.

"Great!" she said. "I'd love the company. I'll pick you up at six in the morning."

"I'll be ready." Frank gave her directions where she could pick him up. It turned out to be a budget motel outside of town. She found it without any trouble. The sun was up and the row of freshly painted white buildings stood out against the small hills of purple and black in the background, an area still in shadow as the sun rose above them.

"Do you want to come in for awhile?"

"No, I need to get to L.A. and make a withdrawal from the bank. We can talk in the car."

Frank shrugged his shoulders, locked the door to his room and dropped his bag in the back seat alongside Lydia's overnight case.

"When we get to your house, it might be best for you to pick up your spare tire."

"Right. That was a mistake leaving it out just to pack a bunch of clothes. I wasn't thinking about having a flat."

"No harm done. You were just out a few bucks, and I take it that was pocket change for you."

The way he said it caused Lydia to wonder. Frank's tone did not seem casual. Still, she didn't find talking about her money to be anything to worry about. Josh had always told her not to talk about money to strangers, but Frank had helped her by dumping Mitch's body, he was hardly a stranger. He had put himself on the line for her, so to speak. *Was that the term people used? On the line?* She knew that trouble could come their way if the police connected either one of them to the dead body. They *were* connected so she might as well get used to having Frank around.

"We'll stop and grab a bite along the way," she said, trying to lighten her mood.

"Fine. I could use a bite. You're treat, right?"

"My trip, my treat," she said emphatically. "Besides, I know you're not working steadily. I don't mind footing the bill at all."

"I guess that makes me a 'kept man' not that I mind it one bit." Frank's smile widened. "I warn you, I'm easy but I'm not cheap."

Lydia laughed at the joke. The trip seemed to take less time than when she'd driven it before. It was nice to have someone along with a sense of humor. Josh had occasionally joked around with her, but his mind had usually been preoccupied with business deals, always looking for angles and suckers willing to yank out their checkbooks so he and Lydia could live the high life. She hadn't minded Josh's ways because she enjoyed their lifestyle, but now with Frank's laid-back attitude, life seemed more fun that with Josh.

When they reached the Bank of Los Angeles West Hollywood on Santa Monica Boulevard, Frank told her he would wait in the car. Lydia hopped out of the Mini Cooper and bounced inside the bank. The teller, who had come up from a branch in Arroyo Grande, paused for a moment when Lydia told her how much she wanted to draw out. But this was the Golden Triangle so the teller knew the bank's customers here probably ran through that much money in a week's time. Still, she needed the approval of one of the bank officers. Seeing the name on the account, the officer quickly signed off on the withdrawal and the teller asked how Lydia wanted the money.

"Large bills, please."

The teller counted out ten thousand in one hundred dollar bills. It came to quite a stack, Lydia thought, but she managed to stuff it inside her bag and thanked the teller before she left.

Frank peeked inside her open bag when she got back in the car.

"Well, you're all set now," he said. "Why don't you show me this fabulous house you live in."

"Say no more. It's just around the corner and up a hill."

Lydia drove to the house and they went inside. She checked her mail. A few bills needed her immediate attention, everything else seemed to be sales papers and solicitations.

While she was looking through the mail, the front doorbell rang.

Chapter 16

MEANWHILE, TRAVELING UP INTERSTATE 5, Vito and Sophia pulled their car up to the Blaine, Washington, point of entry facing the Peace Arch that stands with one foot on the United States and the other on Canada at Surrey, British Columbia. Built in 1921, the monumental gate between the two countries signifies their everlasting freedom and unity. The Fanuccis smiled at the young Canadian border security officer in her crisp dark uniform. The lines of traffic were long. Their son lived in Surrey, British Columbia, and the Fanuccis made a trip twice a year to see him, plus any special trip like this one, to pick up pieces of stolen art for Raymond Atherton.

"Hello, welcome to Canada." The smile was more genuine than it had to be. The young woman was picture perfect as if she were the poster person for the CBSA—Canada Border Services Agency.

"Look, Vito, it's that nice young lady who was here in December," Sophia said and waved at the young brunette with the ponytail hairdo.

"I think you're right, Sophia. How are you, my dear?"

"*Er*—hello." It was clear from the expression on the security officer's face that she didn't recognize Vito or Sophia from any of the other ninety-seven thousand travelers who pass through the various checkpoints each year going to and from Canada and the United States of America.

"Oh, that's okay, dear," Sophia said. "You don't have to recognize us. We're just glad to see you again because it means we're almost to our son's house in Surrey."

"Well, okay. *Er*— do you have anything to declare?" She meant contraband, of course, but Vito's and Sophia's smiles made them look like the quintessential grandparents, not some gunrunners or art thieves.

"Nope," said Vito. "We're just enjoying the fine weather you folks have up here. It's hot in California. Much nicer up here."

The security officer leaned out the large window of her booth and peered inside the Fanucci's classic American Motors Matador station wagon. Although manufactured in 1974, under Vito's careful maintenance the big Detroit bomb looked like it was just coming off the showroom floor. The woman couldn't see anything out of place so she waved them on. "Enjoy your visit."

"Thank you, we will," Vito and Sophia both said together and waved at the officer as they pulled through the checkpoint and headed on their way up Highway 99 to where it intersected with King George Boulevard. Five more minutes and they pulled into their son's driveway.

Pietro lived in a four bedroom house that looked smaller on the outside than it was on the inside. That was due to the heavy landscaping he and his father had done. Tall evergreens grew on both corners of the house, visually squeezing the front portico so the house looked boxy. Junipers grew in a flower bed across the front of the house except where the stoop rose up three steps to reach the front door. The windows in front were dark due to the heavy curtains inside. The white paint was fresh and the reddish-brown shingles were newly placed last summer. The roof arched steeply to aid in repelling snow in the winter and a lone window in the attic was centered between two gabled windows on the second floor.

Vito and Sophia had barely stepped out of their car when Pietro opened the front door and rushed out to greet them. "Momma, poppa…I'm so glad you made it. No problems along the way?"

"Not a bit," Sophia said kissing her son on the cheek. "The weather was beautiful all the way."

"Here, poppa, let me help you with those." Pietro took the two heavy suitcases his father had pulled out of the back of the Matador and ushered them inside the house. "Are you hungry? I have a big pot of stew on the stove or I could slice off some ham if you just want sandwiches."

"Stew sounds good," Vito said. "It's already cooked, you say?"

"Yes, poppa. I cooked it in the crock pot last night, nice and slow."

"That will be fine," Sophia said as Pietro looked at her to see what she might want. "Don't go to any trouble on our account."

"Momma, you are never any trouble. I want the two of you to come inside and sit down and relax. You must be tired. That's a long drive. I'll fill a couple bowls for you and take your luggage up to your room."

He sat the suitcases down by the staircase at the back of the huge, open main room. The room included a large kitchen off to one side where the stairs ran up and over it with their first landing serving as a ceiling for the kitchen. Heavy rough wooden timbers ran across the top of the kitchen's ceiling, each one supported by a set of matching wood timbers that stood upright like table legs. The kitchen appliances were modern and so clean they gleamed with the same brightness and personal care that Vito showed his Matador. Sophia smiled as Pietro rushed through the cabinets to extract bowls and spoons from the silverwear drawer along with napkins and the cut glass salt and pepper shakers which he placed on the breakfast bar in front of them. Sophia leaned over her bowl and drew in a full breath of steam, savoring the richly seasoned smell of the stew.

"Is that okay, momma?"

"Just like I'd made it myself." Sophia smiled broadly at her son. He motioned to his father to take a seat and patted his mother on the shoulder, begging her to do the same.

"I'll just be a minute," he said and picked up the suitcases, hefting them with ease although both were extremely heavy.

The next morning after they had slept, Vito and Sophia came downstairs in their pajamas. Vito smelled the coffee brewing and twitched his lip in disgust. "He cooks well enough," he whispered to Sophia, "but he makes his coffee too weak."

"You hush, old man. You are in your son's house. You will drink his coffee and keep a smile on your face."

Vito did smile, not falsely, not to placate Sophia, but at the humor of it all. Both of them loved their son very much but Vito always compared Sophia to a mother hen or maybe a mother cat every time she was around their boy. Their *boy*. Pietro was old enough to start showing the first sign of gray in his hair. Vito was proud that his son had grown into such a fine man and had made such a good life for himself. All three of them owed their good fortune to Raymond Atherton. Vito had been mostly unskilled when he and Sophia and their then six-year old son had found themselves destitute and in a Salvation Army shelter. Raymond was there to drop off clothing donations and Vito helped him carry the large bundles inside. Raymond had taken an immediate liking to their boy and questioned his parents about their situation. He took them home with him that day. They had worked for him ever since.

After they finished eating, Pietro showed his parents to their bedroom. He'd placed their suitcases on top of the double bed and Vito opened the smaller one. Pietro stared happily at the contents. Stacks of U.S. currency in fives, tens and twenties—all small bills to avoid calling attention to Pietro when he spent the money or deposited it in his bank account—a cool even one hundred thousand dollars, Pietro's part for stealing the masterpieces. There would be more later once the copies were sold to unsuspecting buyers.

"It was a good job, son." Vito clapped a hand on Pietro's shoulder. "Mr. Atherton will be proud of you."

"Please tell him 'thank you' for me and I'll be ready after July to take on another assignment."

"Something special in mind?" Sophia asked with a mother's instinct.

"Yes, momma. I'm going to take a vacation but no, don't get your hopes up, I haven't got a girlfriend yet."

"How am I ever going to be a grandmother if you don't find some nice *Italian* girl to marry?"

"Still insisting that I marry our own kind, huh? You know, I met a beautiful English girl on the way back here."

"English, *humpf*. What do they know except tea and crumpets? You need a nice Italian girl to cook for you and put some meat on your bones."

"Yeah, Pietro, like your mother has done for me." Vito patted his thirty-inch waist, emphasizing how slim he was.

While the Angels Slept

Sophia slapped her husband on his shoulder.

Pietro laughed loudly. "You two get some rest. I'll put this in the safe and we can catch up on everything after you have napped for awhile."

He closed the small suitcase and carried it to his own room where he opened his safe he kept behind the large painting of an English warship in battle against a Spanish galleon. Pietro transferred the cash into the safe, having to jam up the other stacks of bills already in there so he could make room. It didn't matter. He would take a hefty chunk of his earnings to the bank on Wednesday.

Today and tomorrow he would enjoy the visit with his family, then he would give them the six canvasses which they would take back across the border, concealed under the back seat of their car.

Chapter 17

THE FRONT DOORBELL RANG A SECOND TIME before Helen could answer it. She let the two men waiting there inside the foyer and stepped into the breakfast room where Lydia and Frank were having an afternoon coffee.

"Ma'am, there's two policemen here to see you."

Lydia's heart sank and she almost dropped her cup of coffee. Frank sat his cup down hard enough to clink the saucer. The sound echoed throughout the room. He placed a hand on Lydia's arm to steady her nerves and nodded to her as if to say everything would be okay.

"Please show them into the living room," Lydia replied. She looked toward Frank with her mouth forming the word, 'Why?' He shrugged his shoulders and patted hers. They left their cups on the table and walked slowly toward the living room.

Oh, Lord. What will I say?

Lydia put a smile on her face as she walked up to the plain clothed officer with her hand extended. "Hello, I'm Lydia Taylor and this is my friend, Frank Davis." She ignored the policeman in uniform, but was drawn to the detective who seemed somehow familiar to her.

"Lydia? As in Lydia Bradley?" His face showed his surprise. A smile crept across his lips and his eyes opened a little wider taking in

Lydia's total appearance.

"Yes." Lydia said. She hadn't used her maiden name in quite awhile. It seemed strange to hear someone say it. She frowned. "Do we know each other?" She looked at the detective and knew she recognized him from somewhere, but couldn't quite place where they had met until he spoke again.

"Chet Lang, we went to high school together." The detective continued shaking Lydia's hand as he spoke. Realizing how long he had held it, he let go. A smile of embarrassment crossed his face.

"Chet! Oh, my God. How long has it been?"

"High school, I guess. Senior prom. You danced with me when Josh went outside for a smoke. You two got married?" He looked past Lydia to where Frank stood.

"Josh is dead. Automobile accident."

"Oh, I'm sorry, Lydia. I didn't know."

"It's all right. I've come to terms with it already. What can I do for you, Chet?"

"Sorry to bother you, Lydia. I'm with CBI, California Bureau of Investigation. This is Officer Dale Reed, he's with the Highway Patrol. We're investigating a murder that happened just outside of Carmel."

"A murder?" Lydia acted shocked.

"Do you mind answering some questions?"

"No, not at all. Have a seat."

The officers sat down where Lydia had indicated. Detective Lang sat on the sofa. Officer

Reed took a single chair on the side.

"You've been staying in Carmel?" Lang asked.

"Yes, a couple of nights is all. I just got back around noon. How did you know that?"

"We asked around about the victim and was told he left a restaurant with a pretty woman whose car had broken down. We checked with the closest mechanic and he gave us your license tag. We ran it through the Department of Motor Vehicles."

"Yes, oh no, you don't mean Mitch—" She caught herself and smiled inwardly. Her surprise sounded convincing, even to her. *You should win an Academy Award for that kind of acting.* She sat there as innocently as she could waiting for the next question. Frank remained quiet.

"Did Mr. Ryan drive you all the way here to Los Angeles?"

"Who? Was that his name? We never got past our first names. No, I was staying at a friend's place in Carmel. He gave me a lift there."

"Did he stay long?" There was a concern in the detective's voice that made Lydia think his question was more personal than official. After all, she knew he liked her way back in high school, maybe he still did.

"No. I invited him in, but he said something about needing to meet a friend so he left."

"Do you know who this friend was?"

"No, he didn't say."

"And that's the last time you saw him was

when he left there?"

"Yes. You say he was murdered?"

"Looks like it. His wallet was empty, probably just a robbery and the thief stabbed him to keep him from giving a description. The knife was tossed on the floorboard. We're checking it now for prints and registration"

"Oh, my."

Frank had maintained his silence during the questioning. Chet looked at him a moment before asking him if he had known the victim.

"No, can't say that I did. I might have seen him around. Lydia told me he played guitar. I've seen a few blokes playing for sidewalk change, he might have been one of them."

"What do you do for a living, Mr. Davis?"

"I'm an artist. I paint ocean settings, sometimes people."

"Painted anything recently?"

"I paint every day if I can. Actually, I'm a student, trying to do better."

"I see. Well, I guess that's it for now. Here's my card." He handed the card to Lydia and stood up to leave. "Call me if you think of anything."

The CHiPs officer also stood. They left and Lydia fell into Frank's arms. Her body shook all over and tears welled in her eyes.

"Thank goodness they're gone. I couldn't have answered another question."

"You did fine. I don't think they suspect anything."

"I know I should have done the right thing

and called the police when I stabbed Mitch. It *was* self-defense."

"That's right, it was. But you know the cops, always buggering things up. They would have painted you as some kind of trash, leading him to the villa and leading him on, for whatever purpose they could create."

"I'm scared, Frank. I've never been involved with the police or murder or anything like this."

"Just keep your wits about you and stick to your story that he was a kind enough guy who gave you a ride. Keep it simple. The more you say, the more holes they can punch in your story. You're innocent, remember that. Doesn't matter what happened or what we did afterward. Now, where are you going to hide the money?"

She had forgotten about the ten thousand.

"Oh, Josh has a safe. I can keep the money in there."

"And that would be the first place the cops would go for. You need a place where it's not in plain sight but you can grab it quick like if you have to make tracks."

"You mean like an extra purse or something like that?"

"Yes. Anything that will keep it handy, but don't set it out on the table or anywhere that might draw their attention."

Lydia went to her closet while Frank went to the kitchen for another cup of coffee. She came in with a canvass beach bag already stuffed with the money.

"It has a double pocket, see? I can put the money in one side and stuff the other with a quick change of clothes if I need them."

"Perfect. Now, put it in the closet near the front door."

Lydia nodded an okay and Frank followed her to see where she would place the bag. She opened the closet door and crammed the bag onto the top shelf. She thought it looked normal enough up there and Frank gave a nod of approval.

He stood behind Lydia and when she backed up he caught her in his arms. He said nothing but turned her around to face him. Lydia looked at the expression on his face and realized that this might be an awkward moment, but it somehow felt right. It felt right when he pulled her to him and again when he pressed his lips to hers. He kissed her lightly at first, then with a greater passion, letting his tongue part her lips and seek out her own. She responded to him and let him take control for a moment. When his hands moved up from her waist to the outer roundness of her breasts, Lydia drew in a quick breath and pushed against his chest.

"No, wait a minute. I—"

"It's all right. Don't deny yourself the pleasure."

"I—I can't. It's not you. It's…Josh…and Mitch."

"Well, I'm not the one trying to rape you. I simply want us to be together." His right hand cupped her breast as he spoke.

"I know. I like you, Frank. But I'm just not ready yet."

Frank relaxed his grip on her and stepped back.

"Sorry, I didn't mean to push you."

"Maybe…soon. I don't know. Right now, I'm too worried about things. It's all so complicated. Please give me a little more time."

"Sure. I just don't want to lose you."

She smiled and took another step backward. Frank let her go but held her with his eyes. Lydia looked at him and shifted her gaze downward. He had a command over her that she recognized from the way Josh had treated her, and some of the forcefulness that Mitch had exhibited. *Are all men this aggressive?* She didn't remember her father being so forceful at home, only in his business dealings, those she had witnessed at least. To her, he had always been sweet and gentle, as he was with her mother. But she realized that her viewpoint as a child had to be different than what she felt as a woman. Frank was handsome and appealing, but something told her this was not the right time to accept him as a lover.

"Why don't I give you some time to rest," he said, thoughtfully. "I'll call on you tomorrow. We can take care of any business you have and find a quiet little restaurant to go to."

"That would be nice. Thank you."

Frank left. He passed Helen on his way out. She had not seen the newspaper that morning and just now remembered it was probably stuck in the hedge row again where the paper boy seemed delighted in pitching it.

"I keep telling that boy to aim better so I don't have to get stuck by those hedges. I think he does it on purpose." She came inside and handed the paper to Lydia then retreated to the kitchen where she set about lining up the vegetables she would use in a salad for dinner.

Alone in the living room, Lydia started to think about Mitch again. She didn't want to think about the attempted rape or of her shooting him, but she couldn't shake the memories from her mind. She wrapped her arms around herself. Although the temperature in the room was set to a comfortable degree, Lydia's whole body shivered. The house had a starkness about it that she never felt when Josh was around. Her steps echoed from room to room when she walked. Leaving the foyer she returned to the kitchen where Helen was chopping vegetables for the salad. She topped the tossed mixture with sliced smoked chicken breasts and garnished it with bits of pimento and Italian parsley. Lydia dined alone, munching on the salad and slurping a cooled-down spoon of tomato soup, washing everything down with fresh brewed iced tea. She put the dishes in the sink and poured herself a glass of wine to take upstairs to her bedroom. Once there, she kicked off her shoes and sat on the bed. The plush-pile of the soft blue carpet pressed against her bare feet almost like tiny fingers giving each foot a massage. She got up and walked over to the window to look out. She never remembered taking the time to just look out her bedroom window before. Everything with Josh had been rush here, rush there, always on the go. She had never taken the time to simply enjoy the landscape of their neighborhood. The sun was going down and it cast its golden rays across the freshly cut lawn. Lewis stood on the pathway with an edger in his hand adding a finishing touch to the front lawn. He looked up and saw Lydia looking down at him from her window. He smiled and waved to her and she waved back.

She sat down again on her bed thinking about nothing in particular. Her eyes took in the richness of the colors that surrounded her, from the warm burnt-umber paint covering the bedroom walls and the soft lighting that gave them a honeyed accent to the ivory laced curtains over the window and the rich mahogany of the four-poster bed. She stared at the painting above the bed, an eighteenth century oil showing people gathered at a rise above a river, ladies with parasols, men with straw hats and vests, their coats tucked over their arms. A summer outing with children running to and fro in their Sunday best clothing and some of them flying kites. It was a peaceful scene that she had looked at often. She had never envied the ladies in the painting with their babies in their arms. Family life had meant something different to her and Josh. Now, whatever they had was gone and Lydia felt out of place in the world she knew and in the common world so depicted in the painting.

Without realizing the association to her own life, she started singing the song from the play, Annie: *"Tomorrow, tomorrow. The sun will come out tomorrow."*

Chapter 18

THE DOORBELL RANG PROMPTLY AT EIGHT the next morning. Lydia answered the door herself since she had given Helen time off to attend her granddaughter's school play. Lydia was surprised to see Detective Lang standing on her doorstep. This time the Highway Patrol officer was not with him.

"Chet. Good morning. What brings you out here so early?" Lydia face beamed at him, but that was meant to hide the apprehension she felt seeing him again.

"Good morning, Lydia. I wondered if you had a moment."

"Sure thing. Come in. Have you solved the case yet?"

"No, but we've got some pretty good leads. One thing I wanted to check on with you is how you met the fellow who was here yesterday."

"Frank. Oh, my goodness. You don't suspect him of murdering Mitch?"

"Well, I wouldn't go on record. Right now we're just looking at anyone and everyone. How did the two of you meet?"

Lydia ushered him into the living room and sat him down before answering his question. She smoothed out a wrinkle in the dark skirt she was wearing and explained that Frank had worked at a restaurant outside Carmel and how they had stopped at the same location along the highway to gas up their cars and that led to their getting acquainted. She told the truth, not leaving anything out. Like Frank had suggested to her, she kept her answers short and simple.

"So, should I be concerned about him?" she asked.

The detective said, "We have no record on him, not just a criminal record, we don't have a passport or other identity on him either. That's always cause for concern to police agencies."

"Well, he said he was from Australia. He hasn't been here in this country for any length of time."

"That must be true. We're doing a background check. We'll send a query to the Australian authorities and should know something about him in a day or two."

"And what about me? Are you running a background check on me as well?" She laughed.

"Standard procedure, Lydia, because of your association with the deceased. Of course, I already know most of your background since we went to school together. I have to tell you we're more interested in Josh's background than we are yours."

That statement stung Lydia, although she told herself she should be relieved. Her eyes narrowed and a bit more color came to her cheeks. Chet saw that right away and wished he hadn't been so blunt.

"It's not that we suspect Josh of doing anything wrong, Lydia. We just don't have much information on him until he started making headlines."

"Headlines?"

"It's one of the things we're checking on. He had some friends who are…well…questionable."

"I don't know what you mean."

"And I can't go into it right now because it's, *uh,* an ongoing investigation. But we think Josh is…was…always on the up and up."

"Well, that's good to know."

Lydia felt better. As far as she knew Josh had always been greedy, but he was solid all the way. Still, having the police look into their history sent chills up Lydia's spine and she absent-mindedly gazed toward the closet where she'd stashed her money. It seemed to her that Frank had been right about the police and she vowed to keep her guard up on any questions Chet might ask. Old friend or not, he still represented the law.

"I had another reason for coming to see you," Chet said. "It was such a surprise seeing you after all these years and I thought maybe we could catch up on old times."

"Oh, I don't know." Lydia blurted out the words, then thought how suspicious they might sound. "I mean, it's great seeing you again but I have so much to do. I have to see our lawyer about settling some of the business affairs Josh was working on when he died, and I've really got some thinking to do about whether I keep this house or sell it."

"It's a beautiful house," Chet said looking

around. "I can understand what you must feel like not wanting to live here alone now that Josh has passed away. But with today's market, you might be better off holding on to it."

"That's one of the things I have to figure out."

"Well, I recommend a time out at a coffee shop catching up on old times. Remember Marsha Langston? I've got some great gossip on her and I know you know about Dawes Bennet's sex change operation."

"What? No, you don't mean he—"

"Yep! Gives a whole new meaning to the term 'nip and tuck' doesn't it?"

"Oh, my God!" She laughed.

"So, care to join me for a latte somewhere?"

"*Uh*...." She paused. "Yeah, I guess so. How about two o'clock?"

"Starbucks?"

"Just down the block. How convenient. Sure."

"All right. I have some more snooping I have to do but I should be there on time. You have my card?"

"In my purse."

"Get it out and jot down my cell number."

Lydia dug around in her purse until she found Chet's card. She handed it to him and he wrote his cell number on the back then handed the card back to her.

"Just in case I get tied up," he said.

"Fine. I'll see you at two."

After he left, Lydia telephoned Frank but he didn't answer. She then phoned Peter Manning and asked him if there was any paperwork to be signed. She really didn't have anything to take care of that was as important as she'd made it sound to Chet, but she thought she'd check anyway just in case he asked her about it. She also asked Manning for the name of a good real estate agent. She didn't remember who had sold the house to Josh. She hadn't done anything except to sign the paperwork after Josh and the real estate agent had drawn up the papers.

Manning briefly went over some legal matters with her and suggested they meet that Friday. He had meetings planned that would take up most of the week and since the bank accounts had already been transferred solely to Lydia's name she shouldn't need anything else right away.

Lydia tried Frank's number again. Still no answer. She went to the kitchen and sat at the breakfast counter. She nervously clicked her fingers against the counter top as she sat there drinking a glass of orange juice.

One o'clock rolled around, then one-thirty. At a quarter till two, Lydia stepped into the foyer and slipped a scarf around her neck, looked at herself in the mirror to make sure the color didn't clash with the tan colored pants and jacket she had changed into, and walked out the front door. She pulled out of her driveway and headed toward her meeting with Chet. As she turned on the street below her house, a rusty brown truck pulled up in her driveway. A hand-lettered sign on the side of the truck said 'Pool and Patio.' A man in blue striped coveralls stepped from behind the driver's seat and closed the door of the truck quietly. He carried a clipboard in his hand and took his time walking up the stone steps to the front door. He rang the bell and when no one answered, he dropped the clipboard and squatted down to retrieve it. Or so it might seem to anyone watching. What he did instead was produce a lock pick, the kind with a handle like a gun. He inserted the needle point of it into the lock and squeezed the trigger several times causing the needle to bounce up and down. Then he tried the door.

It didn't open.

Frustrated, Frank Davis tried the lock pick again. He clicked the trigger rapidly which, according to the manufacturer, was supposed to bounce the tumblers inside the lock upward until they caught in place. He held a wedge in his other hand, which he could use to turn the chamber once all the tumblers were in place.

The door still didn't open. A gardener next door stepped out of the garage and began watering the owner's lawn. Frank cursed under his breath, retrieved the clipboard from the front step and returned to the truck. He pulled out of Lydia's driveway carefully and drove away at the posted speed of twenty-five miles per hour. Nothing about his actions would have caused concern for the neighbor's gardener or any of Lydia's nosy neighbors. He needn't have worried. Labor vehicles were common enough in rich subdivisions such as Holmby Hills. He would try again later, maybe, with a different set of lock picks. Right now he had a rendezvous with the Fanuccis and Raymond Atherton.

Frank drove the pool and patio truck to a lot on West Olympic Boulevard. The lot was surrounded by a twelve-foot high chain link fence. A small tin building sat on the northwest corner of the lot. It's sliding doors were double locked. There were no windows. Frank parked the truck and retrieved his own car. He relocked the gate and drove back toward Holmby Hills. This time, however, he was headed to the Athertons where a hundred million dollars in stolen art awaited him. The money alone didn't thrill him. Like all crooks, Frank luxuriated in money when he had it. But the biggest thrill for him was the art. Frank's nerves were all on edge as he anticipated gazing upon the work of the masters. Picasso, Matisse, Braque, Modigliani, Léger and Fredrich—only a few of the great painters he had studied all his life. These artists would be hard for anyone else to copy their style but he knew he had the talent. He could do it. He thought about it long and hard, about copying these great works of art. His mind was so preoccupied with his thoughts that he arrived at the Athertons before he realized he was there.

"*Ahhh,* Frank. Welcome." Raymond

Atherton met Frank at the door and ushered him
into the den. The Fanuccis were already there and
seated, waiting for him. Lady Atherton was not
present. She was upstairs in her bedroom. When it
came to business, she never involved herself. She
knew that some of her husband's affairs were a bit
on the shady side, but she placed her trust in him.
He had always been a clever man and he did
everything he could to avoid trouble. Still, she
wanted no part of it. She would wait until
everything was over and done and continue to
support her husband as she always had, the quiet
little wife taking care of the home while her
husband worked to make their life easier and
better.

"Hi, there. How are you?" Frank greeted the
Fanuccis and showed his excitement in the wide
smile he gave them. His eyes were wild looking
as, one by one, Vito carefully unrolled the oil
cloth covering the canvasses and finally the rolls
of art themselves.

"Marvelous," Raymond said. He stood over
the pieces of art spread out across a long table and
bent over them so he could inspect the fine
craftsmanship of each artist.

"Absolutely outstanding." Frank also bent
over the six canvasses but he was looking at
something else. He'd produced a magnifying
glass from his shirt pocket and carefully
examined the texture and colors of the paint
strokes. He checked for cracks in the heavier
smears of paint and looked for wayward strokes

made by the artists that would not have shown up in the lithographs he'd been studying. "Yes, I can work with these," he told Raymond.

The Englishman smiled and draped an arm around Frank's shoulders. Frank pulled back a little, conscious of Raymond's gesture of affection, but not wanting to give the impression that he was homophobic. He would not have wanted to make an enemy of the man who held the purse strings for these great adventures, but neither would he want to encourage any activity that might go beyond their business arrangement.

Raymond stepped back and patted Vito on the shoulder. "Please tell you son the next time you speak to him how happy he has made me with this wonderful present."

"I will, sir. But I am sure he already knows that. Your payment was most generous."

"Well worth every penny, I might say." Raymond studied the paintings again. "Well," he jerked upright rather suddenly, enough so that Frank and Vito took a step backward. "I guess it's up to you now Frank. When can you deliver the first set of copies?"

"As usual, Mr. Atherton, it takes about a week for me to copy one painting. You can't rush something like this, especially if your customers know something about great masterpieces. Besides, you have to let the paint dry. Even with using portable dryers and sunlamps, it's still a delicate process."

"Yes, yes. Quite right. I know all that. It's

just that my customers are rather anxious to get a return on their money."

"The only way I can speed things up is if I mass produce one painting at a time. You know, work on only one; that way I'd be using the same paints and could go from blank canvas to blank canvas and work in layers."

"No, no. Take your time and do it right. Is the studio satisfactory for you needs?"

"Yes, sir. Thank you very much. It's certainly big enough and the skylight is perfect. And Vito has done a marvelous job of landscaping it for me."

Raymond nodded his head at Vito and Sophia smiled at her husband. Vito had done so much to earn Raymond's gratitude. The old man had provided them with a good home and income and had paid for Pietro's education, both the formal schooling and the special training he had gotten from Raymond's friends who were experts in the burglary business. The boy had stayed for awhile in L.A. and had come to adore Raymond as he would a grandfather.

Frank said his goodbyes and took the paintings which Vito had rolled up again and drove away from the Athertons. He stared in the direction of Lydia's house as he drove past on his way to the art studio. He would come back and try again later to retrieve the money she had stored in her closet under his urging.

Chapter 19

LYDIA PARKED HER MINI COOPER in front of Starbucks, removed her scarf and checked her hair and makeup in the rear view mirror one last time before going inside. *This is crazy. I should be avoiding the police.* But something inside of her gnawed at her gut, telling her she should come clean about the atttempted rape and ask Chet for help. He was, after all, still interested in her it seemed. She could tell that from his smile and the way he looked at her, and the invitation to meet him. It didn't sound like being called to the principal's office. It sounded…well, romantic.

She hesitated before stepping out of the car. There was that moment of embarrassment again, a married woman—*a widow*—allowing herself to think about another man.

"To hell with it," she said and opened the door of her car. She opened the door to Starbucks and was immediately overwhelmed with the delicious savory scent of coffee being freshly brewed. Behind that came a wave of cinnamon muffins and something lemony. Lydia sauntered over to the table where Chet waited for her. Maybe it was all the fresh aromas surrounding her, maybe it was the look on Chet's face, Lydia couldn't explain how or why she felt the way she did. She felt alive, although she was doing nothing more than meeting an old friend, which she was, and determined to make it a relaxed and happy meeting. So what if he was a cop with a badge and handcuffs; he was someone who she…trusted.

"Wow! Look at you." Chet stood as she approached his chair.

Lydia smiled, then took note of what she was wearing. She had chosen a tan-colored silk pants and jacket over a yellow-cream blouse. When Chet saw her that morning, she had been wearing a dark skirt and jacket. Her blouse was thin and sleeveless. Somewhere between the house and Starbucks she had managed to undo the top two buttons. Whatever she looked like had met Chet's level of approval; either that, or he was just being a big flirt. He looked up from her chest with a smile on his face.

"I'll take that as a compliment," she said.

"I assure you, it's a well-deserved one," he replied.

"So what are you drinking?"

"Oh, nothing elaborate for me. I guess it's the cop in me. Coffee, black, hot, nothing fancy."

"What's it like being a cop?" She wanted to avoid his questions, so she made small talk instead about his career.

"It's great! Well, not so great sometimes. You run into a lot of low-life, especially here in L.A., especially at night while the angels sleep and the demons come out to play. But now that I've made detective I'm off the streets usually until something really bad happens."

"Like the case you're on now." Lydia bit her

lip. *Why had she asked him that if she wanted to avoid the matter?*

"Like the case I'm on now. That's one of the reasons I wanted to see you again, but I thought it would be better if we met here, sort of catch up on old times first."

"To be truthful," Lydia said, leaning forward across the arm of her chair, "I really don't spend my time talking about old times. There are no memories from high school that I care to revisit. It wasn't a bad time, but it was mostly boring, or just plain unimportant to me now."

As Lydia leaned toward him, Chet took notice again of the two undone buttons on her blouse. It took him a moment to look up again and gaze eye to eye with her.

"Well, it was a pretty good time for me," he finally said. "I met lots of nice guys and gals, many of them are still close friends. But that's all right if you don't want to stroll down memory lane with me. We can talk about what you're going to do now."

"Oh, that's rough waters, I'm afraid." She shook her head.

"That bad?"

"Well, losing Josh still hurts. I can't deny that, but I've already discovered that I have my own two feet and I'm standing pretty solid on the ground, just a little shaky now and then, but I'm getting a lot of support from those close to me."

"It's good that you still have your mom to lean on."

"Oh, *please!* Don't let me mislead you on that one. Yes, she's offered lots of help, but my mom's got other things to do besides take care of me." *After all, she's got her toy boy to play with.* "Besides, I don't really need her help. Our lawyer...I guess I should say *my* lawyer, now...anyway, my legal affairs are in order and Josh left me well taken care of besides the insurance policy."

"That's good. It's a shame you lost him. I liked him, although the few times I saw him at school with you it didn't look like we'd ever be friends."

"Josh had his way about him. He could be a little rough around the edges. I think that was because he grew up institutionalized."

"Yeah, maybe. I guess that is a different sort of life."

"So, besides being a cop, what do you do?"

"You mean, like a hobby or something?"

"Something."

"My life is kind of boring, I guess. I listen to classic rock and roll, work out every day—I play guitar." As he said that, Chet's voice lifted and his eyes widened along with his smile.

"Really? I'd like to hear you play sometime." She thought briefly about Mitch and wondered if Chet had every played guitar at any of the clubs or restaurants where Mitch played.

Chet arose and went to the counter and placed an order for a latte for Lydia. He returned and handed her the drink.

"Did the deceased say anything to you before he left, anything that might indicate who he was going to meet?"

The question came suddenly and Lydia sat back in her chair. She sipped carefully at the steaming liquid and her eyebrows furrowed a moment as if she were trying to recall the conversation she'd had with Chet at the house.

"No. Like I said before, he just told me he had to meet someone; didn't say who."

"Oh, yeah, that's right. That's a cop thing, we tend to repeat our questions. How's you latte?"

"*Um*—good."

"I was wondering, would you like to go out sometime?"

"We are out."

"No, I mean on a real date. Dinner, movie, dancing."

"You dance?"

"Sure, I dance. I've gotten pretty good since high school. I even took lessons at a studio."

"Oh, ha-ha, I didn't mean that to sound like I thought you were a klutz or anything. The dancing policeman...that might be a fun date. Sure, why not?" *Why not?* Frank was fun, but so was Chet. Maybe she should go out with him.

Maybe she should have her head examined. It would be easier if she could just confess everything to him and for him to tell her the shooting was self-defense. Chet didn't seem the kind of policeman that Frank had described to her. He was every bit the old high school friend and seemed to take a personal interest in her. *Could she trust him?* She felt like she needed to. Killing Mitch had been justified, she thought, but having Frank dump his body didn't seem right to her. *If you do the right thing, can't you tell the truth without fear of retribution?* Seems like you should be able to.

"So it's a date then?" Chet asked. "I mean, this isn't too soon after the funeral…."

"No, no, it's fine. Look…don't get me wrong. I loved Josh and still do, but he's not here and everyone from my lawyer to my friends to my dear, loving mother all say that I should get on with my life. That's what I'm going to do, and that means I need to have a social life. I'm not ready to jump into some big romance, but there's no reason I can't go on a date with an old high school chum. So when do you want to go out?"

"How about tomorrow night? Dinner and a movie sound okay to you?"

"It's a start, I guess, but I still want to see those dazzling dance steps you say you've learned. Fred Astaire, Gene Kelly and now Chet Lang."

Chet blushed. When he smiled, Lydia could see dimples in his cheeks. She didn't remember him having dimples in high school, but then, she wasn't all that interested in him back then. She'd had her cheerleading and she'd had Josh. As boyfriends go, Josh was her whole world back then. Well, Josh was gone now and she wasn't a cheerleader anymore. She had time on her hands and she now noticed things about Chet that interested her. Besides his dimples she noticed a few strands of hair stood up straight at the back of his head. He kept running his hand over the top of his scalp to smooth them, so he must be conscious they stood up. His war feathers, she thought, and giggled at the comparison, which caused a questionable look to cloud his face. Lydia patted his hand and the look vanished.

"Dinner and a movie will be fine. What time will you pick me up?"

"*Hmmmm*, I don't know. I mean, I'm not sure when the movie starts. How about I check on that and call you tomorrow about noon?"

"Okay. That sounds good. I'll make sure I don't get hooked up with anyone or anything for the evening and if you call me at noon it'll give me plenty of time to get dressed."

"Sounds fine. Say, did you hear about the art heist? Somebody knocked over a multi-million dollar museum in France. They got away with a Picasso and a Matisse, and a German painting called *Monk by the Sea*."

Lydia immediately thought about the Fanuccis, but didn't want to say she'd eavesdropped on their conversation. She didn't have any proof they'd done anything wrong so she really had nothing to say about them.

"No, I didn't hear. I rarely listen to the news. Are you a big art fan?"

"*Naw*, I'm just a cop and multi-million dollar robberies get my attention. The Canadians put the pinch on some guy up their way today. I guess I'll get a report on it tomorrow. "

"Don't tell me…you're Inspector Clouseau on the trail of the Pink Panther."

Chet grinned, showing his dimples again.

"The Pink Panther was a fictitious rare diamond; this was art."

"Oh, so you're one of those 'get the facts straight' kind of cops?"

"Yeah, I guess so." He grinned again. "Hey, I'm sorry. I wasn't watching the time. Gotta run. They expect me to solve a case or two now and then to justify the fabulous salary they're paying me."

Lydia smiled. Chet was easy going and responsible all in one.

"Go get 'em, Clouseau; or should I say Dudley Do-Right?"

"*Aghhh.*" Chet grimaced, then leaned across the table to leer at her. He squinted his eyes shut tight, drew back his lips and hissed as he spoke. "How about Clint Eastwood as Dirty Harry? Wanna make my day?"

Lydia laughed so loudly some of the other patrons in the coffee shop turned their heads to look at her.

"I think I'll pass on that for now." She laughed again and shook her head. "But save that thought. We might need it later."

Chet's Clint Eastwood look melted into a blush and a smile. He pulled back his chair and stood up. Before leaving he placed his hand on

Lydia's forearm and squeezed it a little. He paused, looked at her with a more serious expression on his face, and impulsively bent over and kissed her on the cheek.

It was her turn to blush, not from the way Chet had acted, but from what she felt inside. A rush came over her which Lydia felt from her cheek where he's kissed her all the way down to her toes and back up. My God, she thought. *I didn't expect that.* She watched as Chet went out the door, watched him wave goodbye to her, and watched him get inside his car and leave. She sipped the last of her latte and felt a chill come over her, although it was a warm day. *I didn't expect that at all.*

Pietro Fanucci moved quickly about the kitchen. He had chopped half an onion and crushed two buttons of garlic, adding both to the sauté pan where he'd already placed four sliced morel mushrooms and three pats of butter. He watched the ingredients sizzle. At just the right moment he tossed in some finely chopped fresh basil and grated some black peppercorn on top. Freshly diced tomatoes completed the sauce and he turned off the flame on the stove. He never got to enjoy the taste of the dish because the doorbell rang and Pietro, uttering a few words of discontent at being disturbed, strode to the door and opened it rather quickly.

"Pietro Fanucci?"

"Yes?"

"You are under arrest."

The next moment was a blur as Pietro was dragged out of the house, handcuffed and placed in a police car. He looked back at his wonderful house and a tear came to his eye. One of the policemen sitting beside him asked Pietro a question but he didn't answer it. The only word he uttered was, "Poppa?"

Frank called at half-past-four that evening. He seemed agitated when Lydia let him in, but he denied that anything was wrong.

"Just an upset stomach," he said. "I get them sometime. Nothing to do with the situation."

He'd said *situation* as if he wanted to avoid saying murder or killing or any of the harsher words describing Mitch's death. That seemed odd to Lydia. Why would Frank feel guilty? Is that what had given him his upset stomach?

"Well, you'd never guess who I had lunch with, coffee actually." Lydia wanted to see how Frank would react to her visit with Chet.

"That cop friend of yours. The one who was here before."

"Y-Yes, but how did you know that?"

"I'm psychic," Frank said and covered the lower half of his face with an arm, like Bella Lugosi in Dracula. His other hand moved toward her in Lugosi's famous hypnotic gesture.

Lydia laughed, but his joke didn't make her feel any better. She wondered if he had been following her. In fact, that's exactly what Frank had done. Ever since his failed attempt to enter her house as a pool and patio person, Frank had kept a watch on her place, hoping for another chance to break in and steal the money tucked away in her closet. He'd seen the detective call on her and he'd seen her hurry away later on, assuming that she was headed for a rendezvous with the man. He'd tried her door and failed to gain entrance. It frustrated him. But when he made his rounds again later in the evening too many neighbors were outside their homes digging in flower gardens or watering their lawns for him to risk being seen entering Lydia's house. He'd had to think of another way to gain entrance without causing suspicion.

"So I came by to see if you wanted to go out with me."

"Oh, and do I detect a little jealously on your part?" She laughed and ran her finger down his chest. "After all, he is an old friend from high school and I barely know you."

"Give me more of a chance and you'll find out how nice a guy I can be."

Frank looked at Lydia in such a way that his expression was both comical and lustily dangerous at the same time. It had its effect on her because she suddenly felt weak in the knees and moved her hand up his chest to his neck, causing him to grab her arms. This gave her the support she needed to regain her composure.

"*Hmmm*, maybe you should hold that thought. Where did you have in mind for taking me out on this gloriously beautiful evening?"

"How about a round of miniature golf?"

"What? I didn't expect that…but it is a great day for it, isn't it?"

Lydia grabbed a scarf to cover her hair and tied it in a knot under her chin. Wisps of her blonde curls dangled out from under the thin material. They walked out of the house down the brick walkway past a double row of pink and purple pansies and Frank opened the car door for her. Being the perfect gentleman wasn't on his mind. He quickly caught Lydia around the waist, turned her toward him and gave her a crushing kiss on the lips. She felt him suck in her lower lip and force his tongue past that, tasting the sweetness of her mouth while closing his hands around her waist and pulling her tightly against his chest.

Breaking the kiss, he said, "Sorry, but you look so beautiful I couldn't resist."

Lydia didn't say anything right away. Her cheeks flushed. She felt the heat rise in her body. She also felt a tremor run up her spine that felt more like a warning than a feeling of passion. She got into the car and waited for Frank to walk around and get into the driver's seat.

"Please don't do that again."

"What? Don't kiss you?"

"I mean, here, outside, in front of the house where the neighbors can see. I'm supposed to be a widow in mourning. I've already broken tradition by not draping myself in black and wearing a veil, except for the day of the funeral, but I'm not supposed to just jump from being a married woman into an affair with another man."

"So you can date your detective friend, but you don't want me to show you any affection."

"It's…it's awkward, that's all."

Frank started the car. "Do you still want to go out with me?"

"Miniature golf? Yes, that's all right. I haven't done that in quite awhile. I just meant…we should maybe not be so public in our…friendship."

Frank shoved the car into gear and drove away. Turning left at the bottom of the hill he headed toward Benedict Canyon Drive. A couple miles later he turned right onto West Sunset Boulevard, then again onto Wilshire Boulevard. When he hit the San Diego Freeway he sang to Lydia along with the Beach Boys tune coming over the radio, *'I wish they all could be … California girls.'* He turned right onto Park Terrace and parked in front of The Putting Green. He was relieved to see there were only a few couples playing the game. To be truthful, Frank wasn't all that interested in miniature golf, but The Putting Green was a far distance away from Lydia's home in Holmby Hills. That gave Frank a clear shot at keeping Lydia close to him while both of them avoided the cop who'd been asking more questions than Frank wanted to answer. If the detective had only wanted to follow routine procedures, why would he have come back to talk to Lydia again? Investigation or romance? Frank wondered what was uppermost on the man's mind.

Chapter 20

THE GAME WENT SMOOTHLY much to Lydia's delight. She was winning. Frank seemed to enjoy it as well, but not caring who scored the least points. He had settled back into his fun mood without any sharpness to his words and without any overtly romantic moves on Lydia. He poked her on the shoulder when she flubbed a hole and hugged her when she made a terrific shot. But his touches were warm, friendly, almost brotherly. She relaxed and enjoyed the game. It wasn't until later when they stopped for a late supper that Lydia's mood changed.

It was the television news that caught her attention and made her start to question Frank's actions. Frank had excused himself and gone to the men's room when the breaking news update came on the screen. An image of the *Monk by the Sea* flashed across the TV monitor and Lydia drew in her breath quickly. It was the same painting she had purchased for twenty dollars from the restaurant operator in Carmel. Not exactly the same, of course, not the original, but her purchase was a darn good copy.

The same painting? Was it a coincidence? She told herself that art students often copied famous works of art for practice. Could this be what Frank had done? Was the guy at the restaurant only thinking the painting was an image of Big Sur because that's what Frank had told him? What bothered Lydia most was the connection between the theft and the conversation she had overheard Vito and Sophia having about art forgeries. Were the Fanuccis really involved with this latest burglary? And was Frank somehow mixed up in it with them? Sophia hadn't acted as if she knew Frank, but what if they did know each other. Wouldn't they keep that quiet from her if there was a crime involved? Of course they would.

Frank returned to the table, still smiling in his jovial way as he had been during their miniature golf game.

"What's up?" he asked, seeing the strained look on Lydia's face.

"Do you know anything about an art heist in Paris?"

Frank's face changed immediately. His gaze shot toward the television screen and his smile vanished. The reporter was still talking about the masterpieces that had been stolen. The corner of his mouth twitched. His eyes narrowed, his nostrils flared and Lydia saw that he had clutched the edge of the table. He glanced around again at the television then turned back to face her. His eyebrows narrowed closer together when he spoke.

"Why would I know anything about an art theft in Paris?"

Lydia didn't answer right away. She looked at him, wondering why his composure had tightened so quickly.

"I just saw it on the news and thought since you are an art student you might have heard the news and paid attention to it, that's all."

Frank's face relaxed. He slumped forward in his chair and his lips pulled back in a bit of a smile.

"Happens all the time in the art world. The *Mona Lisa* was stolen from The Louvre in Paris in 1911. That wasn't for money, it was taken by a patriotic Italian who wanted to return it to Italy, but a lot of the thefts are for money. Paintings are sold to private collectors or held for ransom in some cases. Sometimes a piece or two is stolen by someone who worked at the museum and then got fired, sort of like taking home their own severance pay when they got canned."

Frank said all this rapidly in a pitch higher than his normal voice. His actions made Lydia worry more about her suspicions but she managed to keep her facial expression neutral. She had no proof of anything being wrong. When Frank offered to show her his studio and the other paintings he was working on, she accepted.

They drove back toward Carmel. It was a long ride. The sky had darkened and the coastline had a haze building out on the water line. Frank said he wanted to do some shopping at a particular store just outside of town on the way to his studio. He stopped not at an art store but at a paper and office supply store. Lydia followed him down each isle as he made his selections. Frank purchased two boxes of parchment paper and several sheets of textured art board.

"I'm doing some special paintings," he told her. "The art board here is better than I normally find at an art store."

Frank paid for his materials and they took off again in the direction of Carmel. Lydia sat quietly in the passenger seat not feeling like starting any conversation. Frank did the same in the driver's seat. Whatever he was thinking, and she could tell from the intense look on his face that he was thinking about something, he kept his thoughts to himself until they arrived at an old garage set back from the street and surrounded by a row of hedges. The yard work looked freshly done and decorative with a variety of flowers bounding an inlaid walkway leading up to the front door. The whole design seemed more appropriate for a house than the dilapidated building that Frank called his studio.

Lydia registered her surprise as Frank opened the door. While the building outside looked old and ready for the city to condemn it, the inside was fresh and charming. The walls were painted in bright contrasting colors and decorated with unframed oil paintings and charcoal sketches on eggshell papers.

"What? No Elvis on black velvet?" Lydia teased Frank, who wrinkled his nose and stuck out his tongue at her.

The converted office section of the old garage opened to what was once a mechanic's bay. Frank told her he'd painted the cinderblock walls white to reflect the light coming through a skylight in the ceiling. Six easels stood in the center of the room, each with a covered canvass resting on them. The rest of the room was bare except for the wall nearest the office which held a row of metal shelves where Frank kept his supplies. Chemicals and paint were stored on shelves near a deep well sink at the back of the open bay. As they entered this area, Frank set the papers he'd bought on an empty shelf and motioned for Lydia to come to the center of the room.

"This is what I'm working on now," he said, his face reflecting a serious look. He ripped off the cloth covering the painting and Lydia had to laugh in spite of herself. The painting was a brilliant reproduction of the *Mona Lisa*. Its colors rich and deep with all the beauty and masterful brush strokes of Da Vinci's original. The face, however, was Lydia's. Almost, that is. The features were hers, all right, but Frank had painted her eyes crossed and twisted the lips into something quite cartoon-like. "I hope you'll pardon a bit of humor," he said. "Let's just call it an unfinished work."

"I think it's hilarious," Lydia replied. "That's the way I see myself most days, especially on my bad hair days."

"Well, I had done everything except the face and I was sort of tired when I finished work...I plan to finish it with the real Mona Lisa's smile. Every art student that takes on this project tries his or her best to get the smile just right. It was easier for me to do everything else first so I could concentrate on the smile. I'll paint over it tomorrow and turn it in to my art instructor."

"Not before I capture this," she said, pulling out her cell phone and snapping a picture of the painting, then e-mailing it to her computer at home. "This shot goes on my Facebook page." She laughed again.

Frank smiled, then recovered the painting. He excused himself to use the bathroom, leaving Lydia to roam around the studio by herself. She looked at the canvasses on the other five easels, but nothing grabbed her attention. Most of them had a few marks indicating focal lines and vanishing points, which would become rivers or roads or railroad tracks. She knew enough about art to understand its basic composition.

Two of the canvasses were more developed, showing mountains, trees and grasses. One had a castle lightly sketched into the background.

The last easel had a selection of six sheets of sketches, each with preliminary drawings on them, each in a different style, and each with a completed version of the painting behind them.

The first drawing was nothing but a series of zig-zag lines with the word 'Café' printed in the upper right corner. The completed painting under it was not much better, more colorful of course, but its detail didn't reach out and grab her. The next sketch was a colorful outdoor scene with nude people in it. Lydia thought it looked like something a child might draw, but the profusion of colors made it somewhat appealing.

The sketch on top was nearly as good as the finished drawing, but she could tell that Frank was still working on it. She felt the same about the next painting. It was equally colorful but childishly drawn, she thought. She felt the same thought about all the finished paintings.

The subject of the third painting, if you could call it that, was nothing more than a tree limb. *Why would anyone paint just a limb on a tree?* Lydia confessed to herself that she didn't know anything about what motivated artists and would leave this subject to art students like Frank.

She looked at the last three sketches. In one, she could at least make out the form of a woman holding a fan. The next one was another café scene, full of straight lines boldly rendered around a table with what might be a pitcher of coffee or tea on it. It was the last painting that caught Lydia's attention. The Munk by the Sea. It was only a sketch. The original painting wasn't there. Its absence made her wonder if Frank had already copied the painting and passed it on to the Fanuccis. All that remained was just light markings of a sketch on art board..

"Modern art, huh." Lydia laughed. "You can have it for all I care. I wouldn't give ten bucks for any of these," she said, restacking the finished paintings behind their copies. She had convinced herself that these were only copies, not the originals. Surely Frank, who had been so helpful to her, was just doing what all art students do, copy masterpieces to learn the art.

Lydia looked around to see if Frank had returned. Speaking out loud, she hadn't thought about him hearing what she'd said and now was afraid she might have hurt his feelings if he'd heard her. He must still be in the bathroom, she thought, and hadn't heard her comments. She breathed a sigh of relief and draped the cover back over the sketches.

Lydia passed a trash can and saw that a crumpled piece of paper had landed beside it. *Missed the basket, huh? No place for you on the Lakers team.* She picked up the ball of paper and unfolded it.

She'd intended to toss it in the wastebasket, but she had a natural curiosity and opened the wadded up paper without any real reason. What she found was cryptic.

Another load tonight. Need you to pick it up.

She heard Frank coming back and quickly wadded the paper into a ball again and tossed it into the basket. Frank was looking down at a pencil sketch in his hand so he didn't see Lydia dispose of the paper. He started talking about the sketch he'd just done, but Lydia feigned a headache so she could ask him to take her home.

He didn't seem to suspect anything was wrong; if anything, Frank looked somewhat relieved to end their evening together. He quickly turned off the lights and locked the door and escorted Lydia out to his car, expressing his sympathy for her sudden migraine.

When they arrived, Frank didn't walk Lydia up to her door. He acted as if he had something else on his mind. He pulled out of the driveway, threw a quick wave at her and took off down the hill.

Watching Frank drive away, Lydia couldn't help thinking he was acting strange, or guilty about something.

Something to do with the note and those sketches in his study, it must be. Lydia went to the computer Josh had in his small office off the living room. She was not a computer-orientated person, but she had used them in high school well enough to connect to the internet.

She knew Josh's password, of course, L-Y-D-I-A-1. It didn't take her long to connect to a news page and search for stories about the art thefts.

Lydia looked for images of the stolen paintings. The six sketches in Frank's studio were still fresh in her mind and, call it her intuition, she had somehow known Frank's sketches would match.

She found a page with all of the images on them and knew, even before she clicked on each one to enlarge it, that she had guessed correctly. Lydia saved the page she was viewing, placing it into her favorites file and closed the connection.

Now what? Lydia knew what she was going

to do but her fingers trembled as she picked up the telephone. It took her two more tries before she worked up enough courage to dial the number and listen to the phone on the other end ring four times before someone answered it.

Chapter 21

"CBI, Los Angeles," said the voice at the other end of the line.

"I—I need to speak with Lieutenant Chester Lang."

"Hold please." The line went dead and Lydia wondered if Chet was still working this late. She didn't know if he would come on the line or if he was out and about. She didn't have long to wait.

"Lieutenant Lang, may I help you?"

"Chet...it's Lydia."

"Lydia! Hi, I was just about to call you."

"Chet, we need to talk."

"Sure, what's up?"

"No, I need to see you in person. Can—can you come by the house?"

"Sure thing. Tomorrow okay, or do I need to come over tonight?"

"Now, if you can."

"I'll be there in half an hour." His voice had dropped to a somber tone.

"Good. I've got a lot of things to tell you."

"I take it this is business and not social?"

After a long pause, Lydia took a deep breath and said, "I'm afraid it's business."

Chet's voice lowered even more and sounded quite professional. "I'll be right there, Lydia."

She hung up the telephone and went to the kitchen. She needed a drink. She poured herself a glass of red wine and sat at the breakfast bar waiting for Chet to show. Minutes seemed like hours. She'd finished her glass of wine and looking at the faint pink trace of it in the bottom of the glass, she contemplated pouring another when she heard a car come to a stop in the driveway. She ran to the door to let Chet inside and made a brief greeting, then suddenly the tears came and she burst forth with a string of words that settled on the attempted rape and the shooting.

"There, there," Chet said. He held her in his arms and comforted her. They stood like that a moment, her with her head on his shoulder sobbing gently now that she'd blurted out her story; he, standing there running his hand up and down her back, soothing her as best he could. After awhile, he led her into the living room and sat down beside her, still wrapping an arm around her shoulder and taking her hand in his. He nudged her cheek with his nose and spoke softly to her.

"Lydia, if what you are saying is correct, you've done nothing wrong."

"But, I—I killed him."

"He was trying to rape you. He had a knife. You grabbed it and stabbed him in self-defense."

"You mean you're not going to arrest me?"

"No, not for killing him. I have to let the prosecuting attorney know what happened but I'm sure she'll agree that you were just protecting yourself. There is a problem with moving the body, though. You should have called the police and let them handle the situation."

"That's what I wanted to do, but Frank said...."

Chet held up his hand to stop Lydia from speaking. The tone in his voice was more than just concern for her situation. "Don't say anything else about Mitch. You need to talk to your lawyer. I don't want you to say anything to me without talking to him, just in case I get told to question you officially. Instead, I want to talk to you about Frank and this art heist. What do you really know about him?"

"Not much." She hesitated a moment then added, "I wasn't sure before, but now I suspect that he's mixed up in the art theft that was in the news."

"You're probably right," Chet said. "I have a confession to make. We've been looking hard at him as a suspect. He's a shady character. We think the thief being held by the Canadians is connected to Frank."

"I saw sketches in his studio. They matched the paintings that were stolen."

Lydia led Chet into Josh's study and turned on the computer. She clicked her favorites file and the news story opened. The images sprang onto the screen.

"You saw sketches of these particular pieces?" Chet asked.

"Yes, six sketches he was working on and a finished painting for each of them except for one. He tried to say that art students often copy great works of art to study the techniques of the masters. There's something else; I found a note that was kind of cryptic, it said there was 'another load' coming in. I think whoever wrote the note was talking about these stolen paintings."

"Do you have the note?"

"No, I tossed it in his wastebasket. It's probably still there."

"That's probable cause, the note and the original paintings in his possession; I can get a search warrant if you're willing to testify that you saw all of this."

"Yes—of course, but are you sure all this really means he's a forger?"

"I'm pretty sure he's been doing more than just studying the masters' paintings," Chet said ironically "We can tie that note into the sketches he's done and the finished paintings."

"Oh, my God!" A sudden thought crossed Lydia's mind. "That wasn't just some of Frank's copies I saw was it? The finished paintings he had…those were the original pieces of art."

"That would be my thought," Chet said. "You held millions of dollars in your hand and didn't know it."

"Oh, my…I'm…I'm…I don't know what I am. Shocked? A fool? How could I have been so dumb?"

"Not your fault. You're no art dealer. I'm with you, I wouldn't know a million dollar painting if I didn't see a price stuck on it somewhere. *Uh,* there's something else…I think he's working with an old couple in Carmel."

"The Fanuccis?"

"Interpol gave us a file on the thief the Canadians have in custody. He's well known to international police agencies. Turns out he's the Fanucci's son all right. We're working with the police up in Vancouver and they've agreed to share everything with us. I think it's time we picked up your friend, Frank, and the old couple in Carmel. Do they own the villa in Carmel?"

"No. It belongs to an English couple here in L.A., the Athertons."

"The Athertons? I haven't heard anything about them."

"Lord and Lady Atherton. I don't know if they are involved or not. Lord Atherton deals in antique art pieces, so maybe they are involved, they have a lot of money. They've been good friends to me and to Josh when he was alive."

Lydia fumbled with a doily on a table in front of her. Tears had formed in her eyes again when she mentioned Josh's name. Chet moved closer and once more put his arm around her to comfort her. She looked up at him and felt better. They looked at each other for a long time, then Chet leaned over and kissed her lightly on the lips.

"Don't worry about anything. I'll run a check on the Athertons and see if there's any connection between them and Frank Davis. I suggest you avoid contact with any of them until I get back to you."

"All right." She nodded her head.

Lydia walked Chet to the door and watched him leave. Strange, she could still feel his lips on hers. It was just a simple kiss, not even a romantic one, but she felt it lingering. Lydia closed the door and poured herself another glass of wine.

The next time she saw Chet was later that night at the Bureau of Intelligence & Investigation building in the Los Angeles CBI Regional Office on South Eastern Street. The receptionist paged him and in a few minutes he appeared at the desk in rolled up shirt sleeves and a striped tie, loosely knotted at his throat as if he'd tugged it open earlier and had hurriedly slipped it in place as he came to meet her.

"I'm glad you could come in," he said. "I need you to confirm the people we have in custody are the Fanuccis."

"You want me to look at a lineup?"

"No, just take a quick look and tell me if these are the people you stayed with in Carmel."

Chet led her to a room, stood her before a drawn curtain and hit a light switch on the wall beside the curtain. It immediately pulled back and Lydia saw Vito Fanucci sitting at a table while another CBI agent questioned him. She nodded to Chet that he had the right man. She couldn't hear what was being said until Chet hit another switch and Fanucci's voice sounded through a speaker mounted over the glass window.

"Yes." Vito Fanucci nodded his head.

"Are you sure you don't know anything about any stolen works of art? You don't know anyone creating forgeries?" The CBI investigator leaned over the desk, looking Vito Fanucci squarely in the face.

"No, I don't know anything about art theft except what has been shown on the TV."

"You have a son in Canada?"

Fanucci looked at the agent then slowly nodded his head.

"We have reason to believe your son is part of an international ring of art thieves, and that you know this and that you and your wife are involved."

When he spoke, the old man's voice was firm and heavy with his native accent. "If you had any proof of that, I'm sure my wife and I would already be under arrest instead of just sitting here talking."

"Your son is being questioned by Canadian authorities. As soon as we hear from them we'll decide whether to arrest you and your wife. Right now, I'm just giving you an opportunity to make things easier...at least for your wife."

"Then we should wait and see what the Canadians tell you."

"We are also investigating your accomplice, Frank Davis. He seems to travel quite a bit under different identities."

"I don't know who you are talking about."

"Are you sure you don't know anyonenamed Frank Davis?"

"No. I never heard the name until you mentioned it."

"That's a lie," Lydia whispered to Chet. "Frank spent the night at the villa in Carmel."

Chet looked at Lydia. He said nothing but Lydia wished she hadn't said that; she didn't want Chet to get the wrong idea about Frank and her being alone at the villa.

"He slept in the guest room over the garage," she said. "He joined me for coffee in the main house the next morning before he left. Sophia served him herself."

"Well...maybe we should ask her the same question. It's possible that her husband did not see him, isn't it?"

"Y—Yes, I suppose that's possible." Lydia looked at Vito and wondered if he and Sophia were really mixed up in anything bad. She liked the Fanuccis and hoped they weren't involved, but she remembered their conversation about art and remembered the mysterious note at Frank's studio. She was starting to put two and two together even though she didn't want to believe Vito and Sophia were as guilty as they appeared. Maybe their son in Canada was just a bad egg, but he was still their son so they loved him and tried to help him. Maybe they were just trying to supplement their Social Security pensions because the Cost of Living was just too high for what the government doled out to senior citizens.

Chet thanked her for coming downtown. He escorted her back to the front of the building. Stepping outside with her, he asked for another date but never got around to saying when. Lydia sort of nodded a tacit agreement but both of them found talking about personal matters a little more difficult than talking about the crime at hand.

"I'll call you," Chet said as he stepped back inside.

Chapter 22

LYDIA DROVE HOME STILL WONDERING if the Fanuccis were really involved. She pulled into her driveway and was met at the door by Helen, her housekeeper. After a few words to let Helen know where she'd been, Lydia assured her that she was all right and nothing to worry about.

Helen had placed that day's mail on a silver tray on a table in the foyer, the usual place so Lydia could see it as she entered the house. There were two bills and a notice from Peter Manning, her lawyer, giving her a routine update of Josh's affairs, now hers. Nothing required her immediate attention so Lydia tossed the envelopes back on the silver tray. Helen would move them to Josh's old study out of sheer habit. Lydia had not made any changes in the household routine so Helen would do as she had always done.

Facing a boring day, Lydia jumped on Josh's computer. She wasn't exactly sure of what she was searching for. Anything, she thought, that might make sense of it all. First, she tried a search command on Frank Davis. She got sixty-three million two hundred thousand hits. Too many to go through. She scrolled down the first page and gave up. She tried again by connecting the name with the word art. The results were a little better, only forty-two million eight hundred thousand.

"This isn't getting me anywhere," she

complained.

Next, she tried the Athertons. She typed 'Lord and Lady Atherton' and got a smaller number. There were only one hundred sixty-five thousand hits. She scrolled down the pages and on the third page Lydia found a quick reference to them. Yes, they were bona fide title holders, both of them from Devonshire, England. Their names were mentioned in a newspaper article involving a social gathering at which the Athertons attended. It spoke briefly about Raymond donating money to help needy children.

The second item Lydia found was more interesting. It involved an art sale on May 14, 1990, at which Lord Atherton had sold some charcoal sketches, a collection of practice drawings supposedly by Johannes Vermeer of his painting, *The Concert,* one of about thirty-five known works of art by the great Dutch master. She copied the title of the painting and did a search on just that. What she found was suspicious if not downright incriminating. She found a news story that said the finished painting had been stolen from the Isabella Stewart Gardner Museum in Boston, Massachusetts. The biggest art theft in U.S. history, the painting depicts a woman playing the piano while a man and another woman listen. Lydia read the next couple lines aloud: *"The painting is valued at two hundred million dollars. Thieves broke into the museum at 1:24 A.M. on Saint Patrick's Day, March 18, 1990."*

The story on Lord Atherton said he sold his practice sketches for over a million dollars. *Just two months after the theft,* she thought.

Still, this was not proof that Lord Atherton was an art thief, only that he had acquired sketches of one of the world's greatest masterpieces. What was that he'd said to Josh? *"There is money to be made in the scraps of paper these artists often threw away."* Lydia liked the Athertons even more than the Fanuccis. She didn't want to think Josh's friends were involved in such crimes. It might mean that Josh was mixed up in the affair, although she couldn't believe that, wouldn't believe that, and Chet had told her Josh was not a suspect. She thought some more about the Athertons, especially Lady Atherton. She remembered what Lady Atherton had told her the day of the party, the day Josh died. *"We married well, both of us, didn't we? We must always support our husbands by being there for them."*

Was Josh mixed up in their crimes? She didn't have time to think about it anymore. The doorbell rang. Helen had gone out to shop so Lydia got up to answer the door and was surprised to see, Frank standing there. He looked serious as she stepped aside to let him in.

"Frank. I didn't expect to see you again."

"Yeah, well, I didn't think I'd have to do this."

"Do what? See me again so soon?"

"No, this...." Frank grabbed Lydia and

pushed her aside. He opened the closet door and grabbed the beach bag with the ten thousand dollars in it.

"W—What are you doing?"

"I'm getting out of town and I'm taking this with me." Frank opened the door and was about to step outside when Lydia grabbed him.

Frank whirled toward Lydia and pushed her away from him. She fell to the floor and stared up at him in disbelief. Frank pulled a knife and took a threatening step forward.

"Look, I don't want to hurt you but I will. I didn't want to do it this way but you gave me no choice. You went through the sketches in the studio and found the work I was doing on the stolen art pieces. You knew I was involved with that burglary on the telly. *Crikey*, how did a little dummy like you put two and two together and figure that out?"

Lydia picked herself up, backing a step or two away from the knife Frank held.

"Take the money. I don't care, but please don't hurt me."

"Fine, I don't like violence. You're rich enough you won't miss this." He held up the bag. "To me, this means I can get away to another country, get a fresh start."

Lydia relaxed a little. Frank still held the knife at the ready but he wasn't advancing toward her. He had taken a step backward toward the door.

"Just tell me one thing...are the Fanuccis

involved?"

"Yeah, big time." Frank sneered. "Their son was the one who stole the paintings from the museum. He's quite good, you know. All I do is make copies of the art they provide me and they turn that over to...."

"Mr. Atherton. He and Lady Atherton are involved."

"*Naw*, just him. She knows about things but she's not directly involved. He's the money man. He's behind all of the robberies. He finances the heists and rakes in the profits by selling my copies to his wealthy friends. How do you think he got so rich?"

"I don't believe it."

"Believe it, girlie. That's the way the world works. Those who have lots of money always want more. They're never satisfied. You're rich. It may have been your hubby's money but it's all yours now. In time, you'll be just like everyone else. Money, money, money."

Frank reached the front door and opened it. Lydia remained where she stood. The money wasn't worth getting hurt trying to stop him.

"I wish it could have ended differently," Frank said as he stepped through the door.

"Hold it right there." Chet Lang held his gun leveled at Frank. "Drop the bag."

Frank looked over his shoulder. He saw the gun and how close Lang was to him. Just close enough. Frank swung the bag knocking the pistol out of Chet's hand. He whirled and slashed at him with his knife, narrowly missing the Chet's face. Chet blocked Frank's arm with one hand and grabbed his wrist with the other. He twisted Frank's arm, taking him down in an arm bar. Pressure on Frank's locked elbow caused the Australian to drop the knife. Chet grabbed him by the collar and slammed him into the hood of Frank's car. Chet slipped a pair of handcuffs on Frank's wrists and was lifting the man off the car as two patrol cars screeched to a stop in the driveway, their sirens blaring and lights flashing.

"Take him," Chet told one of the patrol officers.

The officers grabbed Frank's arms and shuffled him toward their patrol car. Chet picked his gun up from the flower bed and brushed some dirt off it before slipping it back inside his holster. He turned to face Lydia and looked at her for a moment before approaching her.

Lydia stood in the doorway with one hand on the facing of the doorframe for support, the other holding tightly onto the doorknob.

"Are you all right?" Chet asked.

"Y—Yes. I'm fine. He didn't try to hurt me, just steal some money."

"You have a mark on your face."

"Well, he knocked me down but that's all."

"Okay. We'll need to take a statement. Come on, I'll drive you and bring you back later."

Lydia stepped back inside the house and grabbed her purse and a wrap. She locked the house and got into Chet's car as he held the door open for her. They drove in silence for a moment before Lydia realized that she had to leave a message for Helen. She pulled her cell phone from her purse, dialed Helen's number and when the housekeeper came on the line, Lydia quickly told her about the events that had transpired.

"Yes, I'm fine. Not to worry." She repeated herself again before ending the conversation. "She's really worried about me."

"I'm sure," Chet said. "You are okay, though?"

"Yes, of course. I'm just not used to dealing with such…such…."

"Yeah, I know. Don't worry. We've got Davis and the Faniuccis."

"And the Athertons? He said they were in it too."

"We'll have to make him repeat what he said to you once we question him. Right now we don't have anything that confirms they are involved. But we'll get them. The report came through on the Fanucci's son. He's admitted getting funding from someone here in L.A., he hasn't shared their names yet."

"They're such nice people. I just find it hard to believe they're mixed up in a criminal activity."

"It's the money. Money does bad things to good people."

"I'm beginning to see that."

Lydia thought about what Chet had said. She thought about how hard Josh had always driven himself to make money. What's the value of money if you aren't happy? Was she happy? She was certainly glad that Josh had left her well taken care of but what meant most to Lydia was peace of mind. She hadn't meant to get mixed up with Frank or Mitch. She realized now that she was reacting to being lost. Without Josh, she had no sense of direction. Lydia resolved that she would do better with herself as soon as this mess was over. And that included Chet. It was nice to meet him again after all this time, but with the way things had been going, maybe she had better stay away from men altogether for awhile.

Taking her statement downtown and letting Frank see that she was going to testify against him brought the whole case to a close, more or less. Frank confessed to everything, including his relationship with the older couples and talked quickly and easily about other thefts. Charges were filed and a judge issued an arrest warrant for both the Athertons.

"I'll take you home now," Chet told Lydia.

"Fine, I'm ready. Don't take this the wrong way but I don't want to see you or this station for some time."

"What about personally?"

She didn't answer.

Chet didn't say much as they drove back to Lydia's place. The streets narrowed and rose higher up through the hills, the grass on the lawns this high up looked greener than the lawns at the base of the highway. Pretty soon Chet made the turn that led up to Lydia's driveway and he parked his car, turned off the engine and turned to face her.

"I guess this mess is over for you now," he said, "that is, until the prosecuting attorney takes the case to court. You'll have to testify."

"Whatever. Just let me know when."

"I will. I—I'm wondering… are we still friends? I know it's been rough on you but the worst part is over and…."

"Chet…to tell you the truth, I think I need a little time to myself right now."

"*Er*—yeah, okay, I understand. This has been a lot for you to handle, what with Josh's death, the attempted rape and now with having to testify against everyone."

"Yes, this has been a bit much. Give me a few days, okay?"

Chet's face brightened. Lydia hadn't written him off completely.

"Yeah, I'll call you in a few days," he said.

He didn't walk her up to the door. Lydia let herself in the house and turned as Chet pulled out of the driveway. She didn't wave, she closed the door, leaned against it and breathed in the familiar smell of what was home to her. Even without Josh, this was still her home. Tomorrow she would devote some serious time to thinking what she was going to do with it, with her life. She didn't want to leave Helen wondering if she still had a job or not. Lydia stepped deeper inside the house. She didn't bother to turn on the overhead lights. Here and there, an accent light gave her all the view she needed. Besides, she knew where each stick of furniture was so she wasn't afraid of bumping into anything.

So it surprised her when she tripped over Lady Atherton's body.

Chapter 23

L ADY ATHERTON LAY THERE motionless in the dark. There was enough light for Lydia to recognize the woman's face and she could tell that Lady Atherton was not breathing. Lydia's hand trembled as she flipped on a light switch. Lady Atherton had fallen half in the living room and half in the step-down dining area. Her eyes were open and her lips had turned blue.

What should I do? Lydia asked herself that question and immediately reached her fingers to Lady Atherton's carotid artery. She had no medical training but she'd watched enough crime dramas on television that she mimicked what she'd seen the actors do. Amazingly, she actually felt a pulse. It was weak, barely a beat or two, but it was there. As she grabbed her cell phone she could see Lady Atherton's eyes move, focusing on her as she called for help.

"Nine-one-one, what is the nature of your emergency?"

"I have a woman not breathing. Her lips are blue. What should I do?"

The operator talked Lydia through the basics of cardio pulmonary resuscitation. Lydia followed directions, giving Lady Atherton thirty rapid chest compressions, pushing down in the center of her chest. She stopped after that and tilted Lady Atherton's head back as the operator directed, then pinched the woman's nose closed and gave her two quick but deep breaths, making sure Lady Atherton's chest rose and fell both times, then she returned to the chest compressions.

She repeated this pattern until the blue faded from Lady Atherton's lips and the woman started breathing on her own. It was a labored breathing but she looked better and managed to mumble a weak "thank you" as Lydia held her in her arms.

A team of medical technicians arrived moments later. Lydia heard the siren and told Lady Atherton not to move.

She rose and ran to the front door, opening it just as two med-techs arrived at the door with a gurney and two carrying cases. One of those, Lydia saw, held medicines and guazes, gloves and the like. The other case remained unopened. Lydia saw markings on the second case indicating it contained a defibrillator. Since Lady Atherton was conscious, there would be no need for it.

As the medical crew transported Lady Atherton to the ambulance, Lydia gave them as much information as she could, which wasn't much since she neither knew whom the Atherton's health care provider was or the name of their medical insurance carrier.

She watched the ambulance roll out of the driveway with its lights flashing and its siren blaring. The siren struck a note inside her brain and Lydia ran back inside the house to find her cell phone. She called Chet's number and waited frantically to be put through to him. She relayed the information as quickly as she could while Chet made notes.

"Which hospital?" he asked.

"Oh, my word. I didn't ask." Lydia replied.

"No problem. I can call the emergency switchboard. What about her husband?"

"He's not here. I haven't seen him. I don't even know what she was doing here."

"I'd better send a car out to their house and see if he's there. Do you have the address?"

"Yes, it's——" Lydia gave him the address and a quick idea of how to get there from her house. Chet listened, then read it back to her to make sure he'd taken it down correctly.

"I'll give you a call and let you know how the lady is doing, and whether we've been able to locate her husband."

"And what hospital they took her to so I can check on her myself."

"Sure thing. You really like her don't you?"

"You mean, do I really like a possible art thief?" Lydia's voice had a harsh note to it. "Yes, I like her. She's always been good to me."

"Don't snap my head off. I'm just being a cop. I do understand that she's probably a very nice old lady so when she's discharged from the hospital we won't throw her in the dungeon, at least not right away."

Lydia relaxed and laughed. Yes, she liked Lady Atherton, but she knew that Chet was just doing his job.

"I'll call you," Chet said again and rang off.

Lydia closed the flip-top of her cell phone and sat in silence in her living room wondering why Lady Atherton had been there. Had she com e to warn Lydia about something? And how did she get inside the house anyway? These were questions to ponder. So, too, did she wonder where Raymond might be.

Lydia surprised herself by speaking out loud. "Surely he wouldn't have left her here to die." She was thinking about Raymond.

She arose from the sofa and went to her bedroom where she changed her clothes. She'd been wearing a light dress, but going out at night, she wanted something warmer to wear.

Lydia didn't exactly know what she was going to do, other than head to the Atherton's house. Maybe Raymond was there. Lady Atherton must have taken a taxi to Lydia's place because there was no car in the driveway other than Lydia's Mini Cooper. Of course, Raymond could have dropped her off.

Lydia had only questions and no answers. She hoped Raymond would be home and she could tell him about the accident. *Was it an accident?* Of course it was, it must be. *Who would have tried to harm such a nice person?*

Lydia grabbed her purse and car keys and headed outside. She backed the Mini Cooper out of the driveway and took the turn at the bottom of the hill and drove the short distance to her friend's house. If Raymond was there, surely the police had already been there and told him which hospital the rescue unit had taken his wife to. Lydia realized that if she couldn't find Raymond she'd have to contact Chet again to find out which hospital to search.

A few moments later she pulled into the Atherton's driveway and parked behind a patrol car. The car's door was open and the officer stood outside speaking into a microphone. He took notice of Lydia and held up a finger as if saying 'wait a moment' then nodded his head at something being said to him by the person on the other end of the conversation. When he was done, he let go of the mike and the coiled line connecting it to the police radio snapped the mike back inside the car. He walked to where Lydia waited inside her own car.

"Ma'am," he started to say something.

"I'm Lydia Taylor. Lady Atherton collapsed at my house. I was looking for her husband."

"I'm afraid he's not here, Mrs. Taylor. At least he's not answering the door."

"Do you know what hospital the ambulance took her to?"

"No, ma'am. I'm waiting on a call about that."

"Mind if I wait with you?"

"Suit yourself, ma'am. I'm supposed to wait here until I get the call. Are you all right then?"

"Yes, I'm fine. Just worried is all."

"Yes, ma'am. Well, if you'll excuse me a moment I'll check in again and see what I can find out."

The officer returned to his patrol car. Lydia wondered why he didn't just use the microphone he carried, the one fixed to his uniform at his left shoulder. She watched as he stepped back to his car and crawled inside. A moment later he returned to her car and said, "Ma'am, maybe you'd better step up to the vehicle and talk to my superior yourself."

Lydia thought he was talking about Chet so she followed him to the car. When they reached the rear door he grabbed her and roughly shoved her into the back seat, slamming the door behind her. The doors could not be opened from the inside although Lydia frantically tried her best to do so. The man jumped into the front seat and started the engine. He shifted into drive and the patrol car leaped forward.

"What are you doing? Are you arresting me?"

"Shut up and sit still, lady," the man ordered as he roared out of the circular driveway and headed off to wherever he was going.

"You're not the police!" Lydia suddenly realized what was happening. Whoever the man was he was not the officer Chet had told her he'd send to find Lord Atherton.

"No, I'm not a cop. I came here to grab the old woman, make her think I was the law and that something had happened to the old man. Don't know how she figured it out. She hit me with a flower vase and ran off down the road. I stuck around looking for the loot from Atherton's last sale but couldn't find it."

"But, how did you steal a police car?"

"*Hah*, that was easy. Check tomorrow's police log and you'll find a rookie spent a little too long on his lunch hour. He even left the keys in the ignition."

"If you're not a cop, who were you talking to on the radio?"

"That? Nobody. I heard you come up the drive and thought that would look official, help me convince whoever you were that I was legit."

"So—so where are you taking me?"

"You'll see. We got the old man tied up, but he won't talk. I think he'll change his mind once he gets a look at you."

Lydia sat back in the seat and quietly took her cell phone out of her purse. *Who said criminals are smart?* She dialed 9-1-1. She covered the sound of the dialing by chatting the man's ears off. She held the phone as high up behind the driver's seat as she dared without letting him see it.

"So you stole a police car and you have taken Raymond Atherton prisoner?" Lydia spoke clearly and a little louder than normal, knowing the emergency dispatcher could hear her. "And now you have taken me prisoner. So where are we going?"

The man had been stupid enough to not take away her purse. Lydia hoped he'd be stupid enough to tell her where they were headed.

"Don't worry about it. We're here already."

"Whittington Lane?" Lydia practically shouted the words into the phone.

"Yeah, we got the old man inside."

"Whose house is this?" She knew the emergency dispatcher was already relaying the information to the police dispatcher.

"My sister and brother-in-law's. He and my sister work for the old couple."

"I know them," she said. "What's their name…Austin, isn't it?"

"Yeah, James and Betty. You can bet James has already softened the old boy up pretty good. When the old man sees you, it'll be just as good as if we had his missus. He'll talk. He's too much of a wuss, not to."

Lydia flipped her telephone shut as the man turned off the ignition. She slipped the phone inside her purse and waited while he opened the back door and pulled her out. He dragged her inside the house and led her to a room in back where his brother and sister-in-law stood guard over a bound and beat up Raymond Atherton. Lydia winced at the condition he was in. Blood ran from his nose and mouth. His left eye was puffy and marked with blood spots under the skin, blue and purple and red where the capillaries had burst. Although severely beaten he was still conscious.

"Oh, my God! What have you done to him?" Lydia ran to Raymond and held his head in her hands. His expression registered how sorry he was to see her, how much danger she might be in.

"Get the hell away from him," James Austin said and jerked Lydia by the arm.

Lydia stood up quickly and slapped Austin in the face. He returned the slap, knocking Lydia to the floor.

"Please, d—don't...." Raymond's voice was weak. There were tears in his eyes.

"Tell me where the money is, you old fart, and I won't hurt her."

Raymond held his silence. He had suffered greatly at the hands of these three. Lydia hoped they would not hurt him again.

"Tell me what I want to know, you old bastard, or I'm gonna beat the crap outta this beautiful lady. And if that doesn't make you talk," his voice lowered as he leaned closer to Raymond, "I've got a few other things in mind for her."

The other man laughed and grabbed Lydia around the waist pulling her roughly to him.

Raymond's eyes narrowed as he looked up at the man. "Don't hurt her." His voice was firm and commanding.

"Or what," Austin said with a sneer.

"Or I'll kill you," Raymond said.

Something about his voice made Austin's voice run silent. Lydia also drew in her breath at the firmness in Raymond's voice and manner. Bloody as he was, there was a strength in the man that made him sit straighter and a fire in his eyes that burned viciously into Austin's.

"Yeah, right," Austin said. He had seen

Atherton's moods change course before. Being tied up didn't seem to phase the old man. He had lived the life of an adventurer so Lydia figured Raymond had faced greater dangers than this in the jungle. But what could he do all tied up? She hoped the police would arrive soon. Surely the emergency operator had heard all of the conversation in the car. *Didn't she?* Surely Chet would lead the charge coming up to the house.

"Nice try, old man." He grabbed Lydia and pulled her away from the other man, pulled her close to him, one hand around her throat. He pulled a combat knife from his back pocket and flipped open the blade. It opened with a harsh clicking sound and Austin brought it up dangerously close to Lydia's throat.

"D—Don't," Raymond pleaded. His passive demeanor returned. His facial expression registered the fear he felt.

"Last time, tell me where you've hidden the money or I start slicing this pretty lady's face."

Chapter 24

RAYMOND OPENED HIS MOUTH to speak but before he could say anything, the door burst open and officers in SWAT uniforms stormed into the room, their assault rifles aimed at the three suspects.

"CBI, put the knife down!" Chet stepped forward. He held his pistol at eyeball level and stopped with the barrel of it less than two inches from Austin's face. Austin's wife and brother-in-law raised their hands in quick surrender. "Do it now," Chet ordered. His mouth twisted into a perfect imitation of Clint Eastwood's most intimidating sneer. His eyes remained cold and focused on the man. His hands held the pistol rock solid steady.

Austin dropped the knife and the SWAT team rushed forward taking all three perpetrators prisoner. The SWAT commander nodded to Chet when the shackles were snapped into place. He motioned to his men and they removed the prisoners.

Lydia felt weak in the knees but very thankful this ordeal was over.

"You okay?" Chet asked her.

Lydia fell into his arms and said, "Thank you."

"Me? If anyone's the her here, you are. You did a heck of a job calling the 9-1-1 switchboard. How'd you come up with that?"

"It was the only thing I could think of doing," she said.

"Pretty good thinking, I'd say."

She looked up at him and saw him smiling down at her. She rested her head on his shoulder and let him hold her.

One of the SWAT members cut the ropes holding Raymond Atherton in the chair. A med-tech rescue team moved forward and checked his bruises and vital signs. They cleaned his wounds, applied a bandage to his head and nodded to Chet that he was going to be all right.

The SWAT officer helped Raymond stand.

Chet let go of Lydia, holstered his weapon and stepped in front of Raymond.

"Mr. Atherton, you're under arrest."

Lydia shook her head at Chet's declaration but Raymond motioned to her and shook his head back and forth.

"It's all right, Lydia. It's what has to be. What about my wife?" Raymond turned back to face Chet.

"She's already in custody," Chet said. "I'm afraid she's a little shaken up but she's fine. She's in UCLA Medical Center. She was at Lydia's and wasn't breathing. Lydia performed CPR on her and called the EMT. We have a female officer with her. As soon as the doctor releases her you'll be able to see her at our headquarters."

Raymond nodded his head at Chet to signify that he understood. He turned to Lydia forcing his bruised and torn lips into a half smile. With tears in his eyes he whispered a 'thank you' to her. The SWAT officer holding him upright handcuffed him and led him out of the room.

"Chet...." Lydia started to say something.

"We've got to question them, Lydia. We'll take it easy with them but we have to treat them like any other suspects."

"I understand. I know what they've done but they have been very good to me. Don't be upset but I'm going to call my lawyer and have him represent them, at least for the time being. They may have another lawyer, but right now they need someone on their side."

"Wouldn't have it any other way. They're not violent; they're just thieves and forgers and scam artists. These other three, we're going to throw the book at them."

Lydia nodded her head and pulled her cell phone from her purse. She called Peter Manning and explained the situation to him. He told Lydia he'd send someone to CBI Headquarters. Manning explained that he wasn't a criminal lawyer, but he had a close friend who was. Lydia thanked him and closed her phone, dropping it back it inside her purse.

She felt better. As she and Chet stepped outside, the sun wrapped around her like a mother's arms. Puffy white clouds filled the sky, each with a touch of gray that hinted it might rain. It wouldn't matter if it did. Lydia was happy to put everything behind her. She was ready for a fresh start again.

Chet's hand lingered on her shoulder as he guided her toward his car. *He's nice,* she thought, *really nice.* But she assured herself that she would take things a little slower from now on. Dinner and a movie, maybe; a day at the beach, and—oh, yes—those dance steps he'd learned. Lydia breathed deeply and let the air out slowly. She smiled as Chet opened the door for her and she got inside.

"We have to get the paperwork done, first," he said as he settled himself behind the wheel, "but once that's done, and you have time to relax a bit, I think we should go out on a real date, not just a coffee shop."

"That would be nice," she said.

Chet smiled. A moment later his smile turned into a grin.

"What?" Lydia asked.

He shook his head. She looked at him with the question still hanging between them but Chet said nothing. He was obviously happy, but whatever it was he kept it to himself. They pulled into a parking lot behind the CBI building and he held the door open for her as she got out.

Two hours later the paperwork was done and Chet offered to drive her home.

Lydia walked past a room and saw Raymond talking to a forty-ish something man in suit and tie. The man turned and saw Lydia, waved her over and introduced himself as Stuart Windsor.

"Peter Manning sent me," he explained. "I'm going to represent the Athertons."

"Oh." Lydia's eyebrows arched. "What will happen to them?"

"I'm afraid that's up to the prosecuting attorney. I've already called her. She gave me the impression that she would be interested in a deal if Lord and Lady Atherton cooperate. You know, provide evidence and testimony."

"What about the Fanuccis?"

"Do you want me to represent them as well?"

"Yes. If you don't mind."

"It's a bit strange, having the victim helping the criminals. Are you sure this is what you want to do?"

"I don't feel like a victim, at least, not with them. Frank is another matter, he tried to steal from me, and the other three, they tried to kill me, well one of them did anyway. But Raymond and his wife, Vito and Sophia, they were good to me and I don't think they would have done anything to harm me."

"*Hmmm,* okay. I'll do what I can to lump the cases together when I meet the prosecuting attorney. If the Fanuccis will offer testimony too, then I think we can keep the charges down, maybe even get some kind of light sentence and probation because of their ages."

"Do what you can."

Lydia excused herself and stepped deeper into the room. Raymond's face was a mess where Austin had worked him over, but he managed a smile as Lydia approached him.

"I'm glad you're all right," he said. "And

thank you for Mr. Windsor. I'm afraid all my funds have been frozen and after this case is adjudged, I'm afraid there will be precious little for Mumsy and me. After prison, I mean."

"Well, it's only fair," Lydia said. "Taking care of you, I mean. You were responsible for turning so many investors toward Josh. We...I wouldn't have the money I do without your support these past few years."

"Josh was a good boy. I was happy to help both of you. I assure you, I never included your husband in any of my...sideline ventures."

Lydia smiled. She had never thought her husband was involved with anything wrong. It was reassuring to hear Raymond confirm that.

"Are you ready to go?" Chet said behind her.

"Yes, I'm ready."

Lydia leaned down and gave Raymond a hug and a kiss on the cheek.

"I'll look in on Lady Atherton," she said, patting his hand.

"Thank you." Tears clouded Raymond's eyes. His smile was weak but Lydia knew he appreciated her kindness.

"Home or hospital?"

"Oh, I think I'll go home first. Just drop me off and let me get some rest. It's late. I'll go by the hospital tomorrow. Right now I need some sleep."

"Home it is." Chet pulled out of the parking lot and headed toward Holmby Hills. He pulled into Lydia's driveway but she didn't get out of the car.

"I want to know something. Why were you grinning at me back there?"

"Me? Grinning at you?"

"Yes, you were grinning. What were you thinking?"

"Well, it's about you and all those paintings at Frank's studio. You held hundreds of millions of dollars in your hand and didn't know it, remember?"

"Like I'll ever forget that. I can't believe how dumb I was."

"Not so dumb when you think about it. More like dumb luck. Don't you realize there's a reward out for those paintings. Rewards are usually around ten percent so that makes you about a million dollars richer than you were this morning."

"A million dollars? You've got to be kidding me."

"Well, it's true I don't know the exact amount, but I'm listing you in my report as the person responsible for locating the stolen art. That should take care of any lawyer's fees you incur for defending the Athertons and Fanuccis without ever touching your current bank account. You're a pretty good detective. Not bad for an ex-high school cheerleader who never graduated from business school."

Chapter 25

THE NEXT MORNING, Lydia dressed casually in jeans and light pink blouse with a yellow cardigan tied around her neck. She stopped at a gas station to fill up the Mini Cooper then headed to UCLA Medical Center, which was only a short drive away. She remembered hearing about her neighbor, the pop superstar Michael Jackson, being rushed there during an afternoon that she and Josh were going to the Athertons for one of their parties. Jackson was pronounced dead on arrival. Lydia wondered if she had seen the ambulance.

Also known as the Ronald Reagan facility, the one million-plus square foot, ten-story structure sits on four acres at the southwest corner of Westwood Plaza and Charles E. Young Drive South. Lydia bypassed the latter entrance where she knew trauma patients were usually taken and skipped the valet parking. She parked the Mini Cooper in the massive lot off the south entrance leading to 757 Westwood Plaza. She marveled at the wide corridors and startling interior design. *Josh would have loved this building,* she thought.

The lobby was a massive open walkway. Natural light filtered through huge glass windows. Soft overhead lighting reflected off the highly polished tiled floors. Lydia strolled past the Meditation Room and seating area and headed to the information desk and the east elevators.

While the Angels Slept

A receptionist checked on Lady Atherton's status and directed Lydia to Level 7, the Cardiac Observation Unit. Lydia proceeded to the east elevators and rode up quietly, wondering how Lady Atherton was doing.

"It's *dysrhythmias*," Lady Atherton told her. "The doctor said my heart was a freight train on a fast track." She laughed. "I told him, 'You try getting attacked and see if your heart doesn't go into overdrive.' But the good news is I don't have a history of heart problems in my family.

"I was planning on a walk around the block when that ugly man showed up at my door pretending to be a policeman. I fooled him, hit him on the head with a vase of flowers and took off on a run. I felt a little dizzy and out of breath from running so far and I was staggering a little when I reached your driveway.

"It's a good thing I was wearing my fanny pack with my keys in it. I have a passkey to your place that Josh provided us when he first bought the house. Anyway, I managed to get inside before I fell down. That was just moments before you found me. I'm ever so grateful for what you did, saving my life and all."

Lydia patted the woman's hand and told her she was happy to see her alive and well.

"They'll be letting me out today…but…ah, I won't be going home."

"I know," Lydia said, again patting Lady Atherton on the hand. "I spoke to the police lieutenant. I also saw Raymond. He's in custody, but he's all right. He sends you his love."

"Oh, what a mess we made of things, didn't we?"

"I hired a lawyer to represent the two of you."

"Oh, my dear. You did that for us?"

"You and Raymond have always been kind to me. It's the least I can do."

"I want you to know, at no time did Raymond or I ever include Josh in our business dealings. He was like a son to Raymond. We would never have hurt him nor you."

"It's all right. I'm sure both of you cared for us."

"How—how are you doing? Without Josh I mean."

"I'm fine. I'm getting along. I'm learning to stand on my own two feet."

"I'm happy for you, then. Oh, this is my doctor."

A rather pretty woman in hospital blues approached Lady Atherton and looked at her chart. She gave a polite hello to Lydia as Lady Atherton introduced her to the doctor. A quick check of her vital signs and the doctor smiled at Lady Atherton.

"I guess we won't be seeing you anymore. You're fit enough to go home. Just too much anxiety. I recommend a long week of relaxation and no running away from bad guys. Save that for the movies."

"I never watch movies," Lady Atherton said. "Too much violence."

While the Angels Slept

A nurse appeared with a wheelchair and Lydia stepped out of the way as Lady Atherton eased herself out of bed and into the chair. "I'll look in on you later…downtown." Both she and Lady Atherton looked sad-like as they said their goodbyes. Lydia left the room, stepping past the uniformed officer who waited outside the door to escort Lady Atherton to jail.

"Will she be able to see her husband after she's booked?"

"Yes, ma'am. Lieutenant Lang has arranged for them to visit awhile before she goes into the female detention center."

Lydia turned toward the row of four elevators and pushed a button. A bell sounded faintly and one of the doors opened. Lydia rode it downstairs, walked briskly past the seating area and out the door into the bright sunlight, walking past the hospital's Dream Garden to the big parking lot. "They need Vito to do something to that garden," she said to herself.

She felt much better now that she had made arrangements to help her friends. Both the Athertons and the Fanuccis would be represented in court. Both would take their punishments, but because of their ages and because they would be witnesses for the prosecution, their punishments would be less severe than the others involved.

Lydia would still have plenty of money left over to get on with her life. *What kind of a life would that be?* She wondered. Well, she thought, for one thing, she had decided not to sell the house. She would tell Helen as soon as she could so the woman would not have to worry about finding another job.

And there was always Chet. She promised herself to take life a little slower, but Chet was a nice guy and...*hmmmm*, she didn't know that much about him after high school. It might be fun to learn what he's been up to besides being a police officer and a dance student.

She unlocked her Mini Cooper and pulled out her cell phone. Chet answered on the first ring.

"About that date you had in mind," Lydia said. "Let's go dancing."

Acknowledgments

As with many writers, I draw from the headlines of various newspapers and other sources to add authenticity to my stories. For this story I wish to thank the Guardian.co.uk News, The Los Angeles Times, The New York Times (Europe) for details of the real museum robbery that I used as a basis for this story. Also TripAdvisor.com for a check on the weather in Paris the night of May 20, 2010, Google Maps for a map of Paris and British Towns Network for a map of England and attractions near Dungeness Lighthouse. I also wish to thank the following members of The Penpoint Writers Group, Sherwood, Arkansas, for listening to various passages of this story and for making suggestions. Those include Harlain Ruff, Debbie Lincoln, Jennifer Lafferty, Glenda Hughes and Layne Flemming. Also, I thank the various members of the Fiction Writers of Central Arkansas who participated in the critique of this work, primarily John Eichler, Darrell Tessman, Jim Bell, Ken and Dee Forrester, John Achor and James Eades

About the Author

Photo by Codi Bogard

DEL GARRETT grew up in Galveston County, Texas, and graduated from the Department of Defense Information School of Journalism in 1979. He took post graduate courses in 1981 at the University of Oklahoma. His feature stories have appeared in international magazines. His first fiction, a Civil War story, was published in Louis L'Amour's Western Magazine in 1995. His short stories have also been published in Pro Se Presents, Blood Moon Rising, GateWay Science Fiction, and Storyteller Magazine. WHILE THE ANGELS SLEPT is his first mystery novel. He lives in Judsonia, Arkansas, and is active in two writers groups and the annual Arkansas Writers' Conference. He is available for speaking engagements, contact him on Face Book.

www.authorsden.com/delgarrett

Also Available From Raven's Inn Press

TEXAS JUSTICE—*A crooked politician and his gang of killers are gobbling up ranches in South Central Texas. When a retired lawman kills an outlaw in cold blood, the opportunity to settle an old score is too much for the gang leader to resist.*

*****

WHISPERS IN THE WIND—*Chief Inspector Lionel Diggins of Scotland Yard has one more case to solve before he retires ... he must catch Jack the Ripper.*

*****

SHADOWLIGHT—*Sometimes a newsman sticks his nose where it doesn't belong. But how else would Rio Shannon get the girl of his dreams?*

*****

FLEA MARKET TALES—*A collection of award winning short stories and previously published stories.*

223